[redacted]

TIGER MOTH
AND THE
DRAGON KITE CONTEST

Librarian Reviewer
Diane R. Chen
Library Information Specialist,
Hickman Elementary, Nashville, TN
MA in LIS, University of Iowa
BA El Ed & Modern Languages/Chinese,
Buena Vista University

Reading Consultant
Mark DeYoung
Classroom Teacher, Edina Public Schools, MN
BA in Elementary Education, Central College
MS in Curriculum & Instruction, University of MN

STONE ARCH BOOKS
MINNEAPOLIS   SAN DIEGO

Graphic Sparks are published by Stone Arch Books,
151 Good Counsel Drive, P.O. Box 669,
Mankato, Minnesota 56002.
www.stonearchbooks.com

Library of Congress Cataloging-in-Publication Data
Reynolds, Aaron, 1970–
    Tiger Moth and the Dragon Kite Contest / by Aaron Reynolds; illustrated
by Erik Lervold.
    p. cm. — (Graphic Sparks. Tiger Moth)
    ISBN-13: 978-1-59889-056-3 (library binding)
    ISBN-10: 1-59889-056-5 (library binding)
    ISBN-13: 978-1-59889-229-1 (paperback)
    ISBN-10: 1-59889-229-0 (paperback)
    1. Graphic novels. I. Lervold, Erik. II. Title. III. Series: Reynolds, Aaron, 1970–
Graphic Sparks. Tiger Moth.
PN6727.R45D73 2007
741.5'973—dc22   2006007701

Summary: Fourth-grade ninjas Tiger Moth and Kung Pow have fun with their classmates
celebrating the Chinese New Year. Tiger's rivals, the Fruit Fly Boys, enter the kite-flying
contest and the result is sky-high disaster.

Art Director: Heather Kindseth
Designer: Keegan Gilbert

1 2 3 4 5 6 11 10 09 08 07 06

Printed in the United States of America

TIGER MOTH AND THE DRAGON KITE CONTEST

BY AARON REYNOLDS

ILLUSTRATED BY ERIK LERVOLD

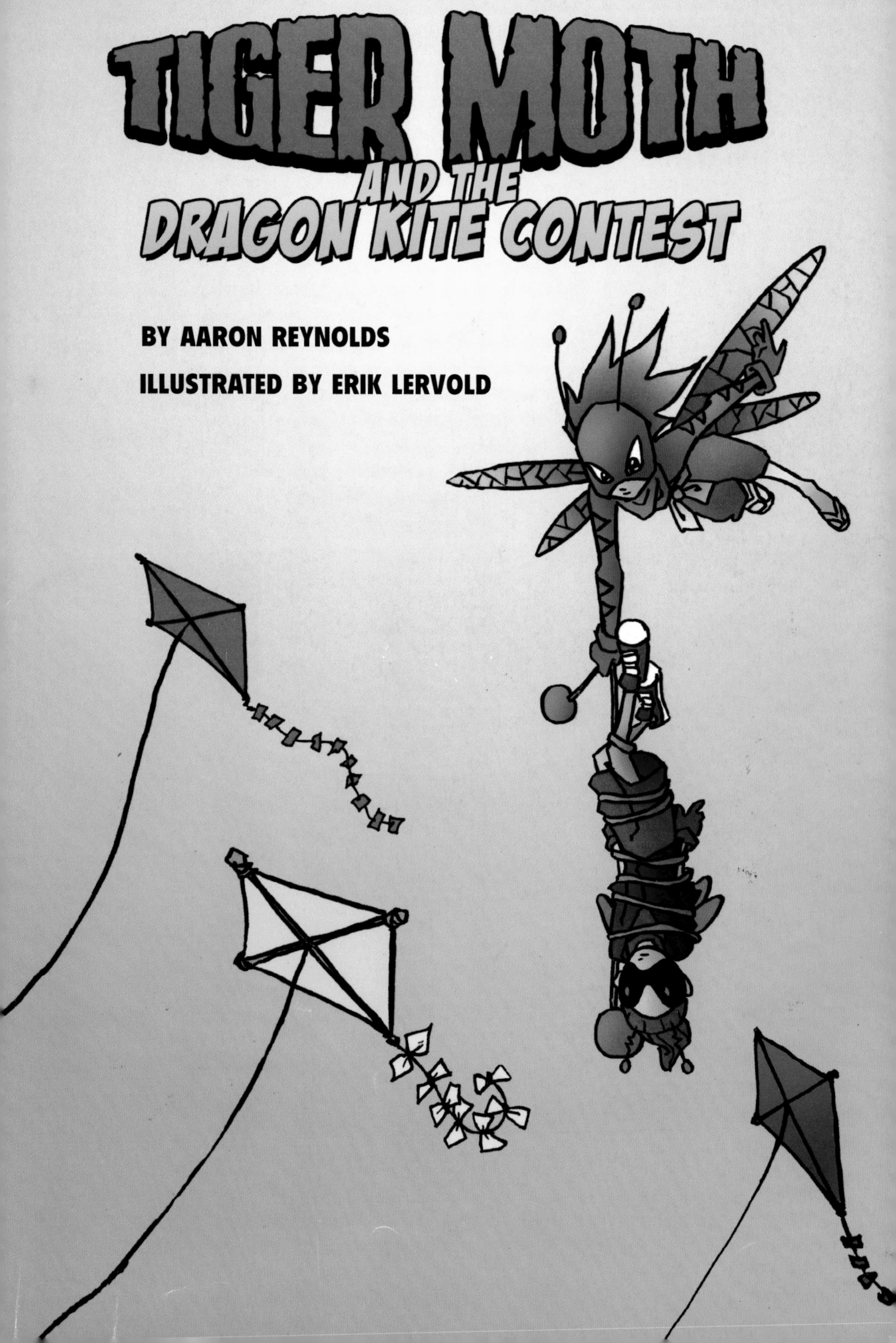

CAST OF CHARACTERS

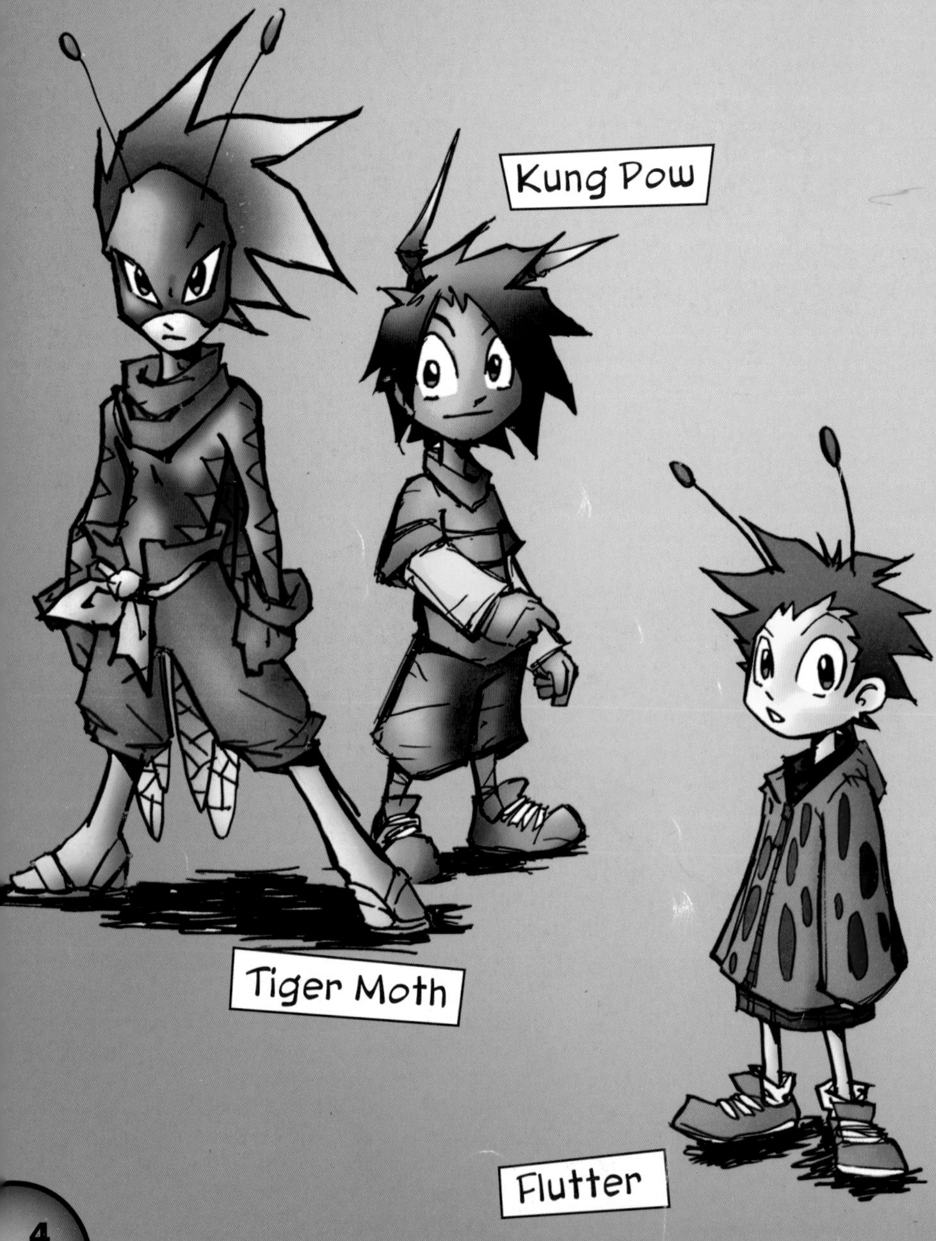

Kung Pow
Tiger Moth
Flutter

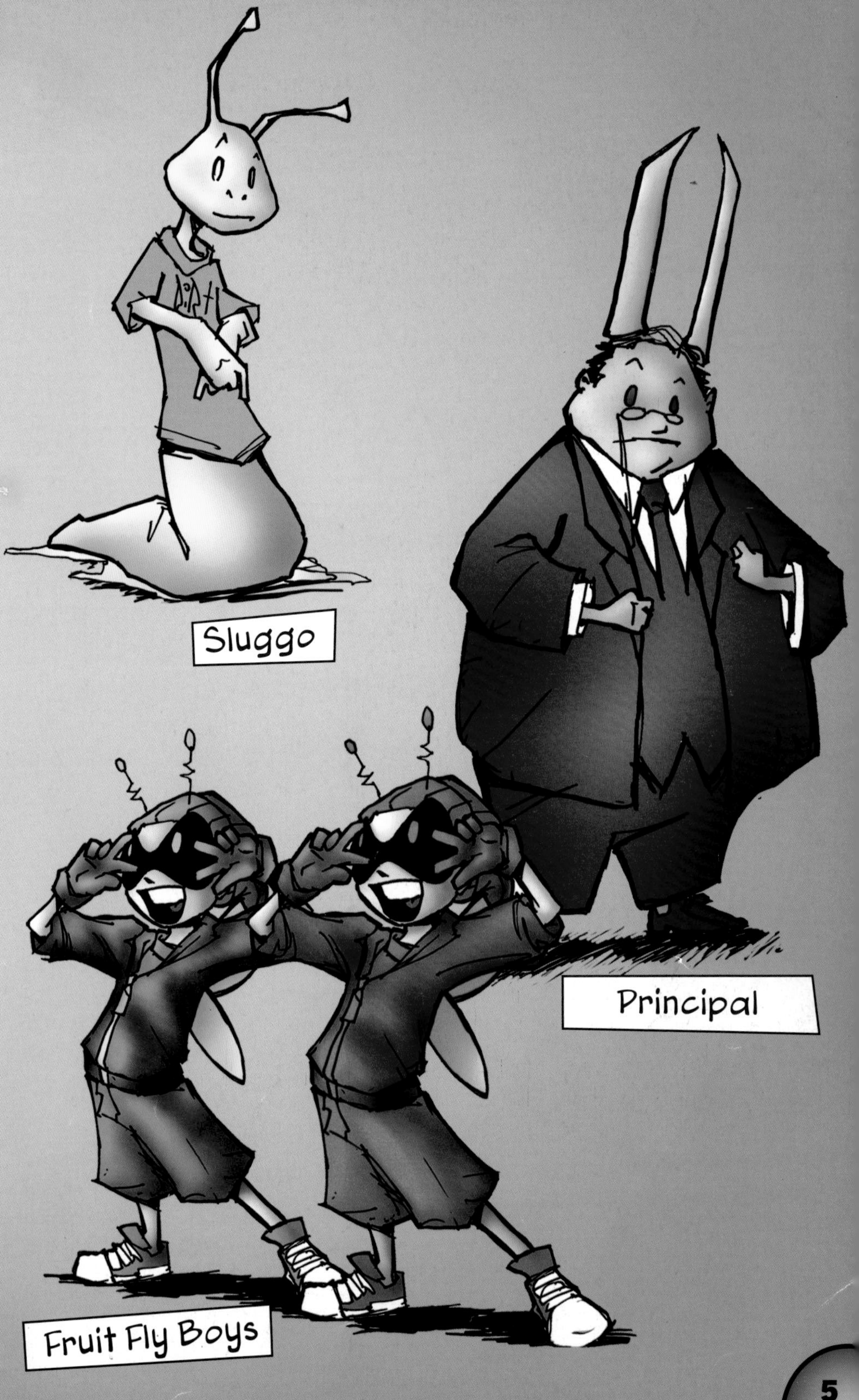
Sluggo
Principal
Fruit Fly Boys

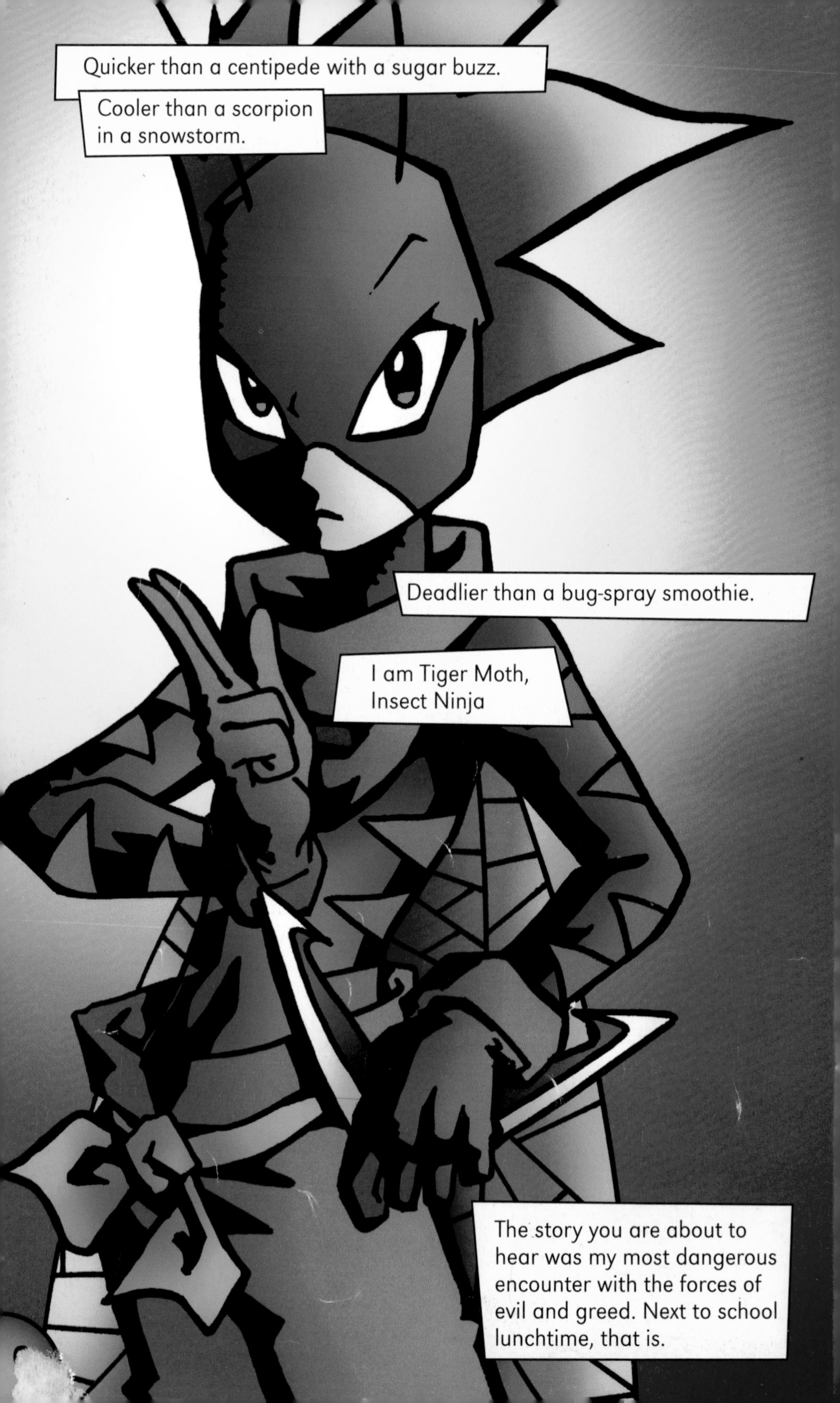
Quicker than a centipede with a sugar buzz.
Cooler than a scorpion in a snowstorm.
Deadlier than a bug-spray smoothie.
I am Tiger Moth, Insect Ninja
The story you are about to hear was my most dangerous encounter with the forces of evil and greed. Next to school lunchtime, that is.

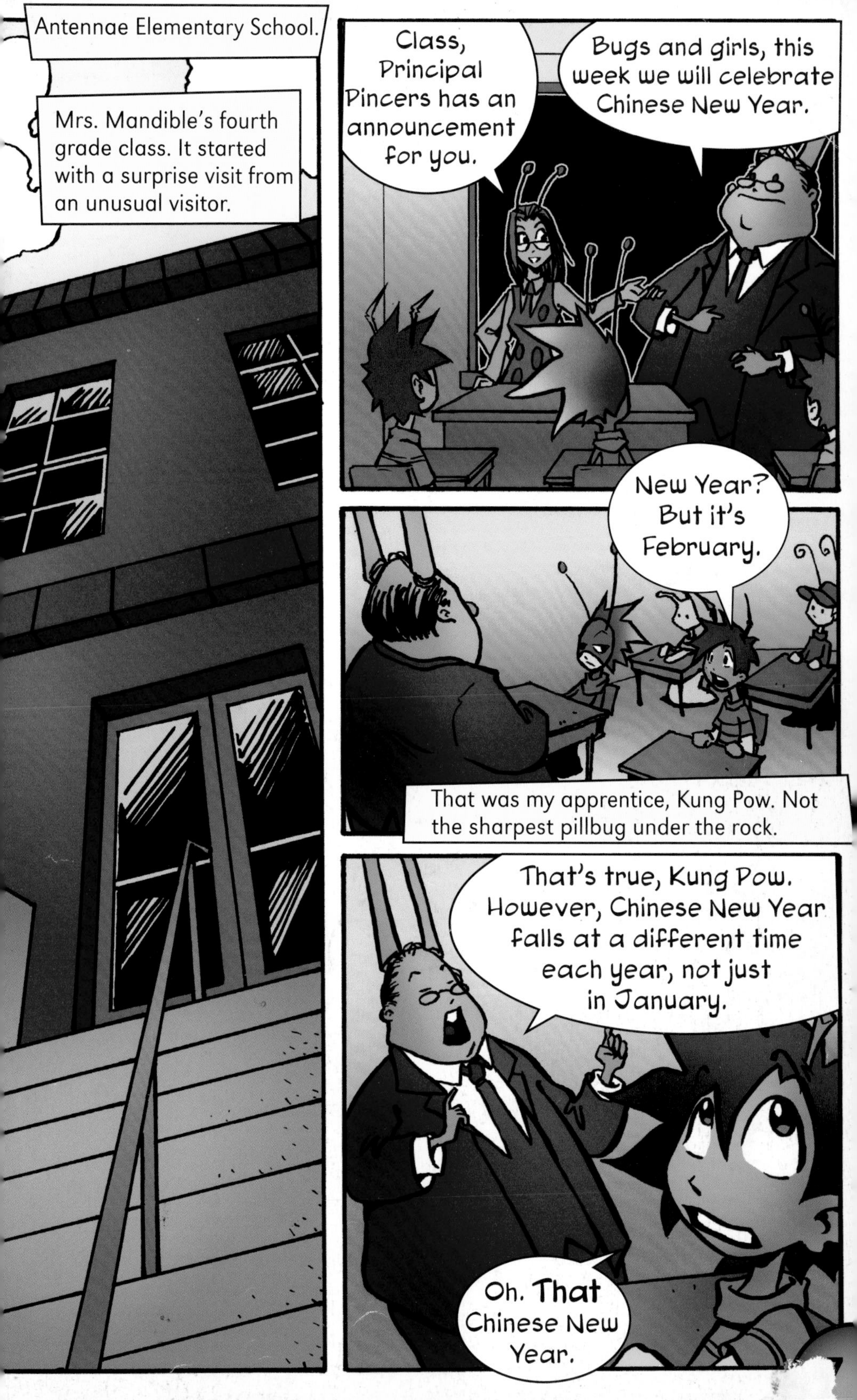

Antennae Elementary School.
Mrs. Mandible's fourth grade class. It started with a surprise visit from an unusual visitor.
Class, Principal Pincers has an announcement for you.
Bugs and girls, this week we will celebrate Chinese New Year.
New Year? But it's February.
That was my apprentice, Kung Pow. Not the sharpest pillbug under the rock.
That's true, Kung Pow. However, Chinese New Year falls at a different time each year, not just in January.
Oh. That Chinese New Year.

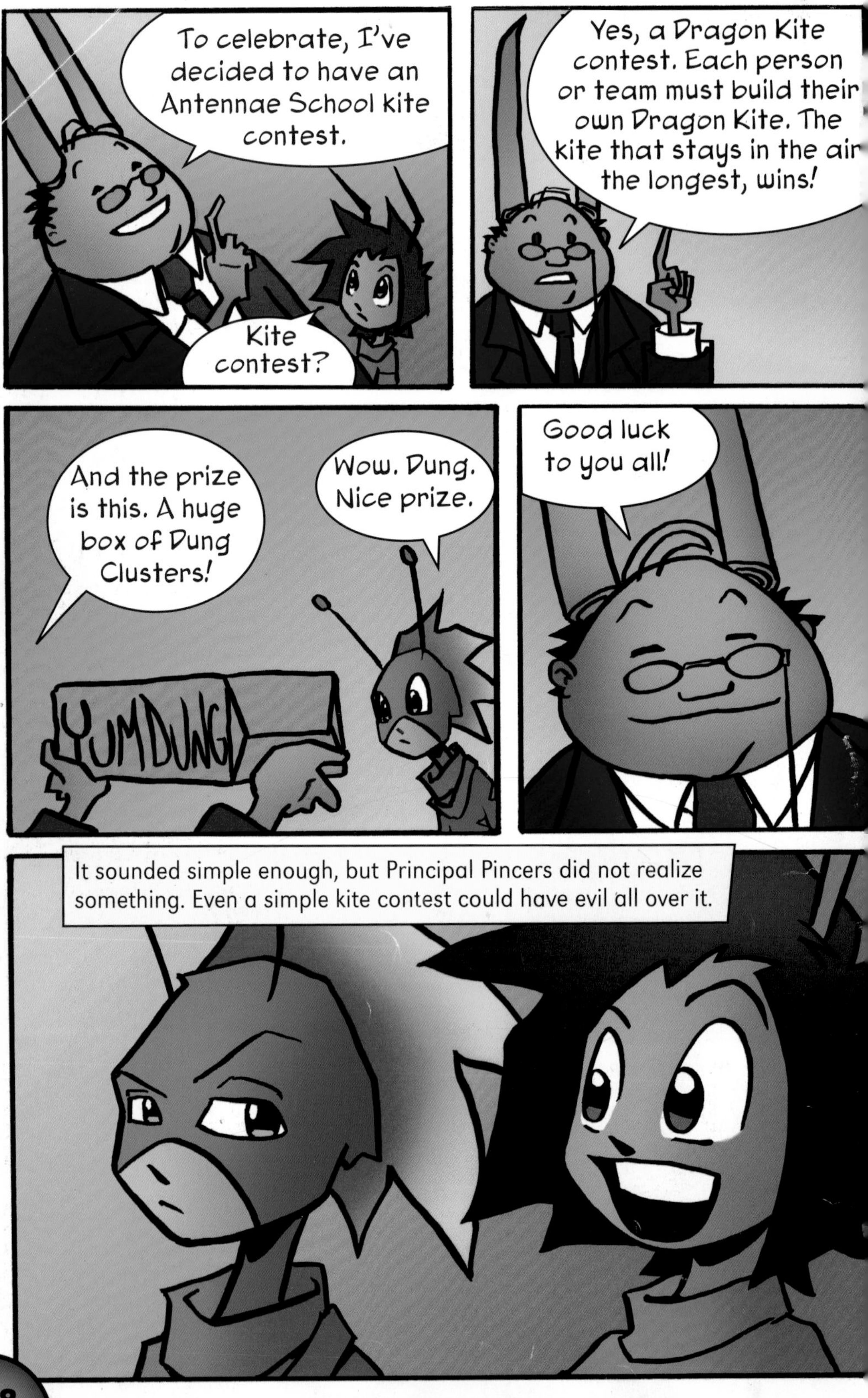
To celebrate, I've decided to have an Antennae School kite contest.
Kite contest?
Yes, a Dragon Kite contest. Each person or team must build their own Dragon Kite. The kite that stays in the air the longest, wins!
And the prize is this. A huge box of Dung Clusters!
YUMDUNG
Wow. Dung. Nice prize.
Good luck to you all!
It sounded simple enough, but Principal Pincers did not realize something. Even a simple kite contest could have evil all over it.

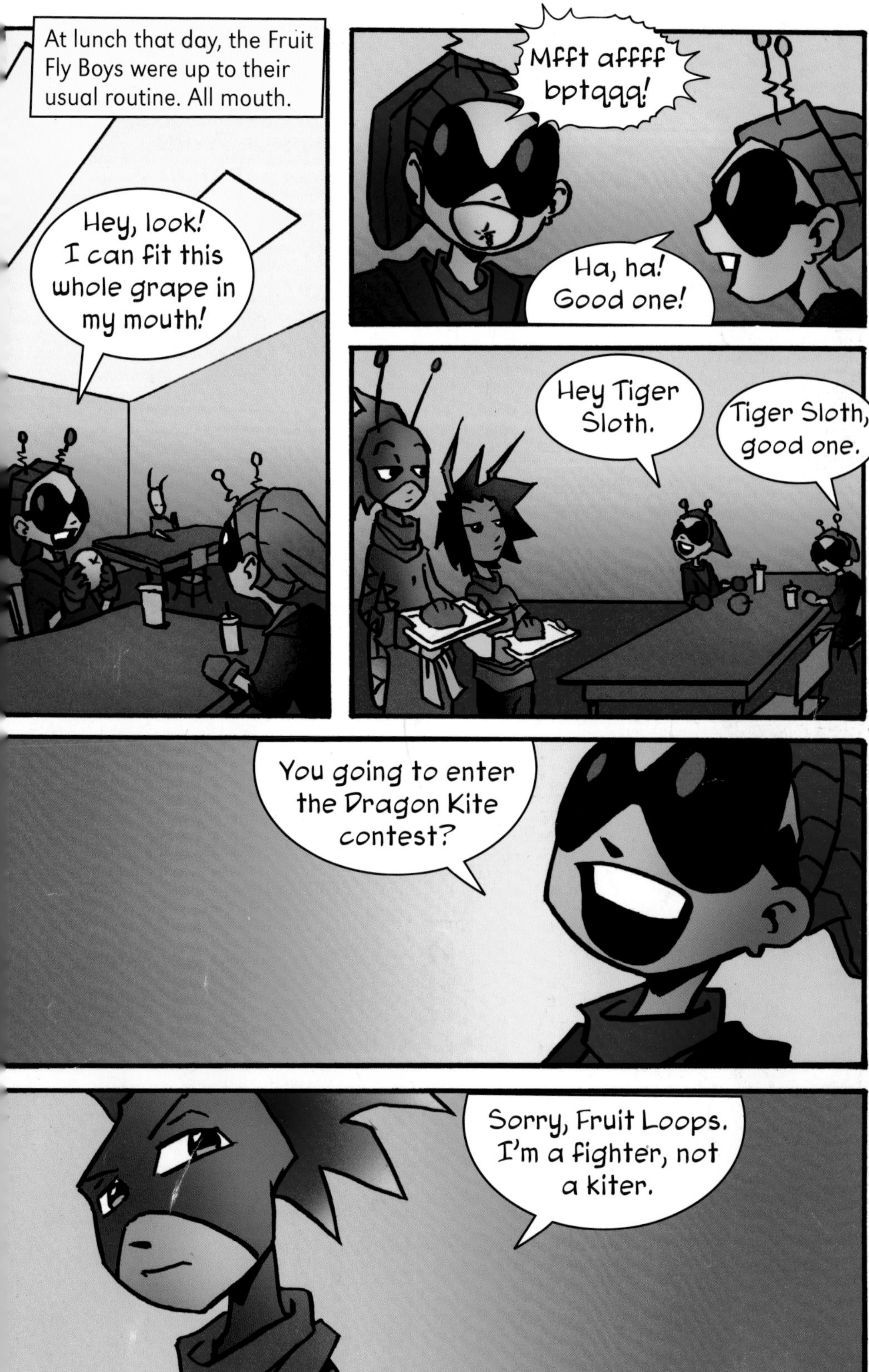

At lunch that day, the Fruit Fly Boys were up to their usual routine. All mouth.
Hey, look! I can fit this whole grape in my mouth!
Mfft affff bptqqq!
Ha, ha! Good one!
Hey Tiger Sloth.
Tiger Sloth, good one.
You going to enter the Dragon Kite contest?
Sorry, Fruit Loops. I'm a fighter, not a kiter.

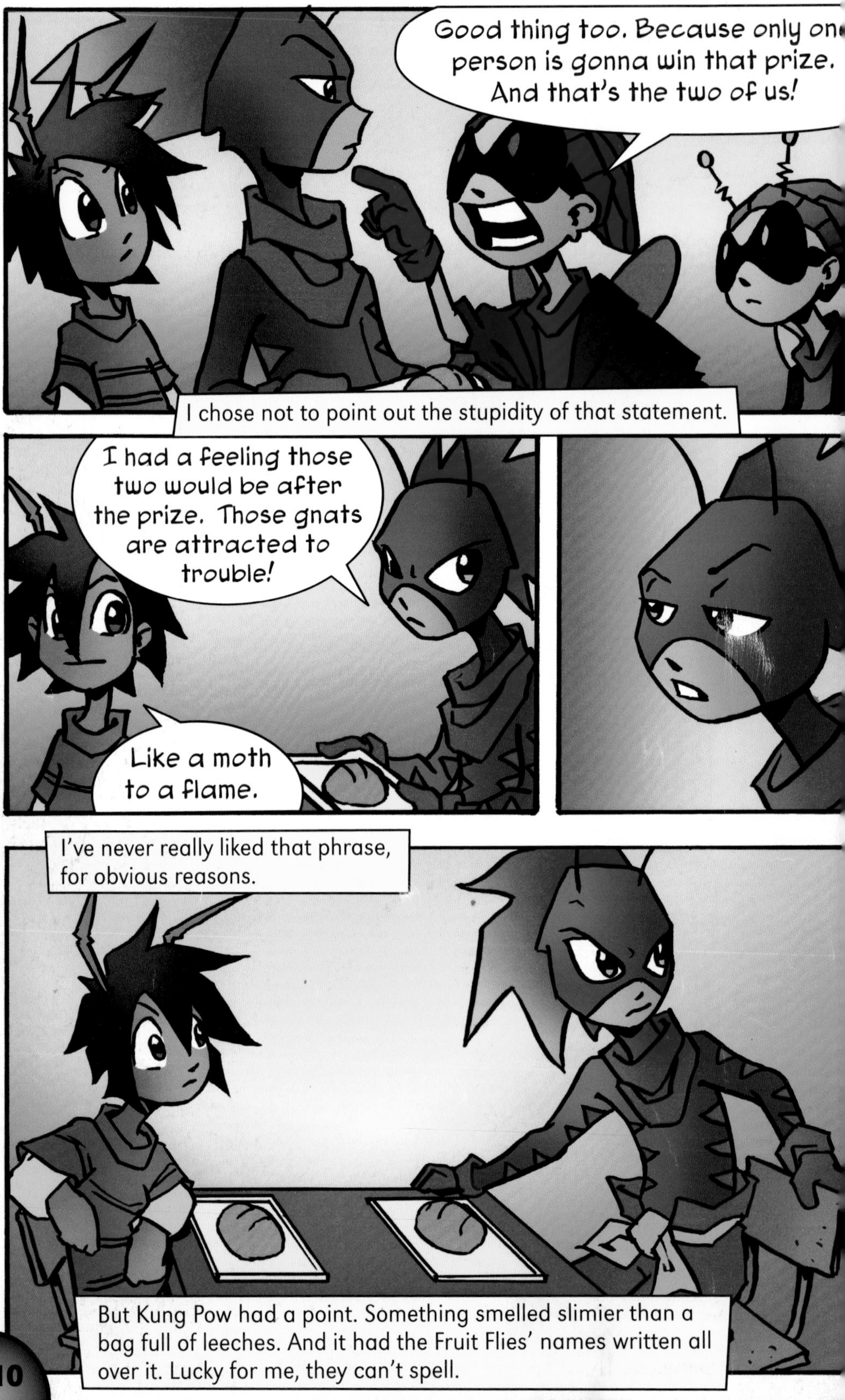
Good thing too. Because only on
person is gonna win that prize.
And that's the two of us!
I chose not to point out the stupidity of that statement.
I had a feeling those two would be after the prize. Those gnats are attracted to trouble!
Like a moth to a flame.
I've never really liked that phrase, for obvious reasons.
But Kung Pow had a point. Something smelled slimier than a bag full of leeches. And it had the Fruit Flies' names written all over it. Lucky for me, they can't spell.

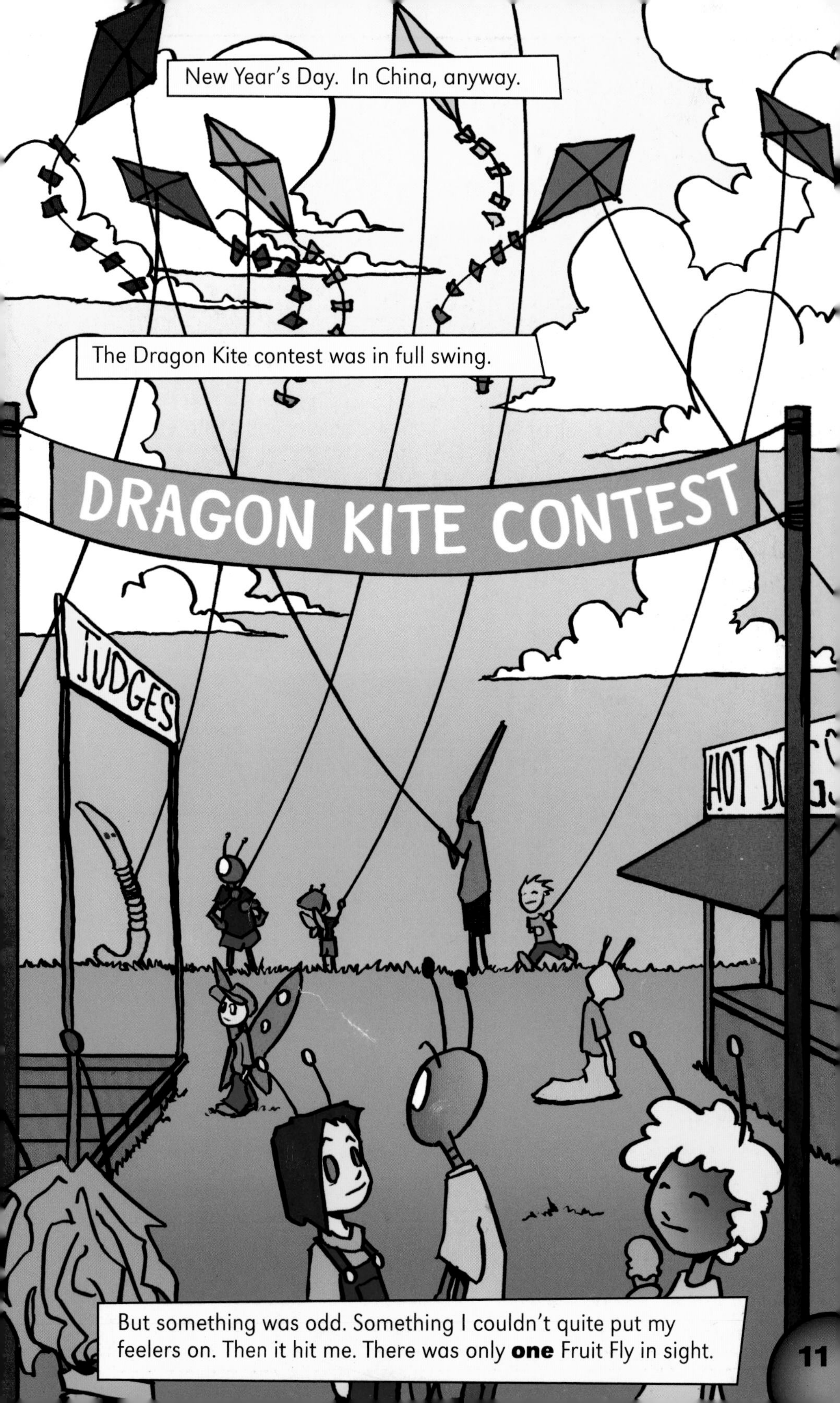
New Year's Day. In China, anyway.
The Dragon Kite contest was in full swing.
DRAGON KITE CONTEST
JUDGES
HOT DO
But something was odd. Something I couldn't quite put my feelers on. Then it hit me. There was only **one** Fruit Fly in sight.

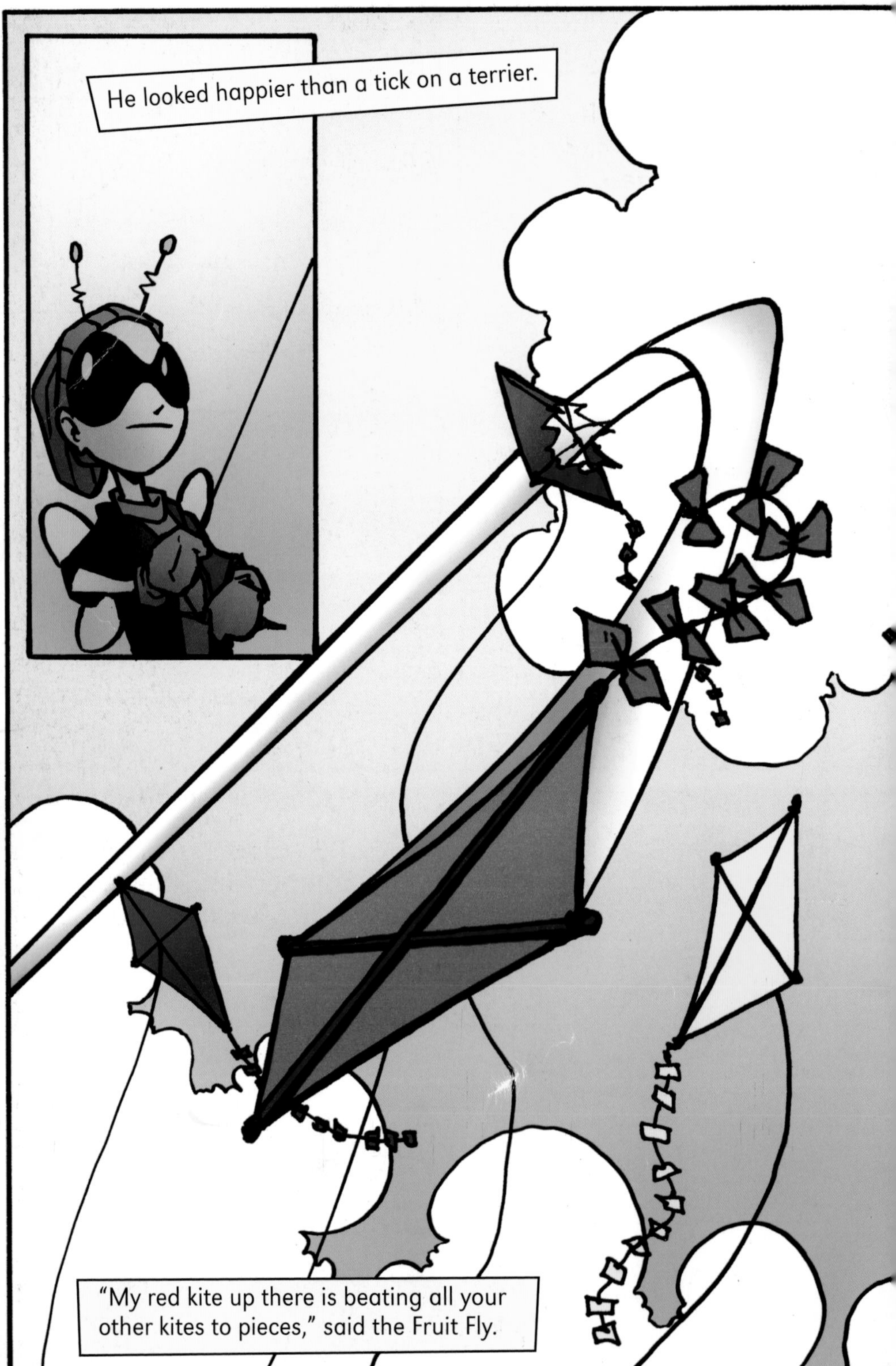
He looked happier than a tick on a terrier.
"My red kite up there is beating all your other kites to pieces," said the Fruit Fly.

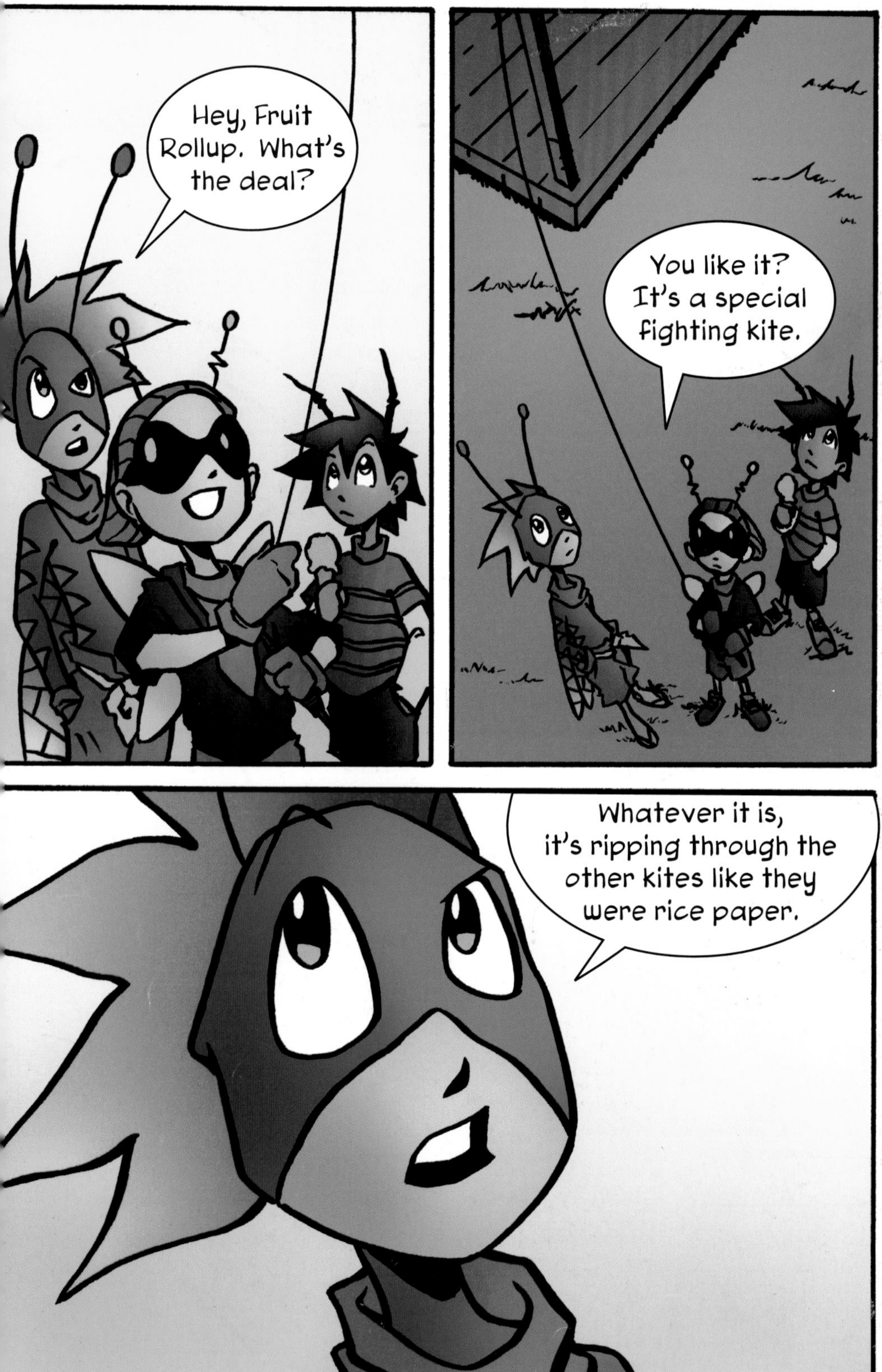
Hey, Fruit Rollup. What's the deal?
You like it? It's a special fighting kite.
Whatever it is, it's ripping through the other kites like they were rice paper.

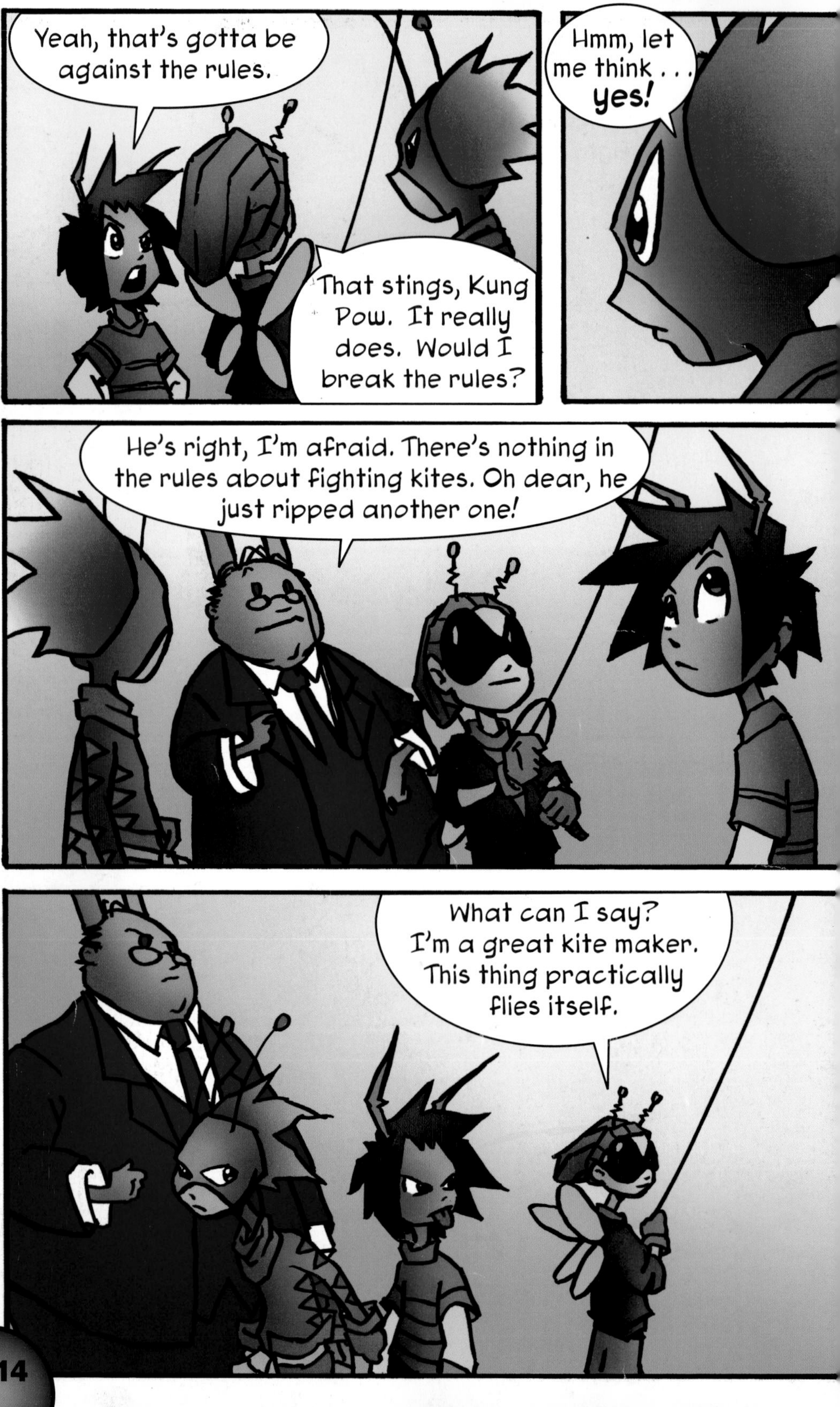
Yeah, that's gotta be against the rules.
That stings, Kung Pow. It really does. Would I break the rules?
Hmm, let me think . . . yes!
He's right, I'm afraid. There's nothing in the rules about fighting kites. Oh dear, he just ripped another one!
What can I say? I'm a great kite maker. This thing practically flies itself.

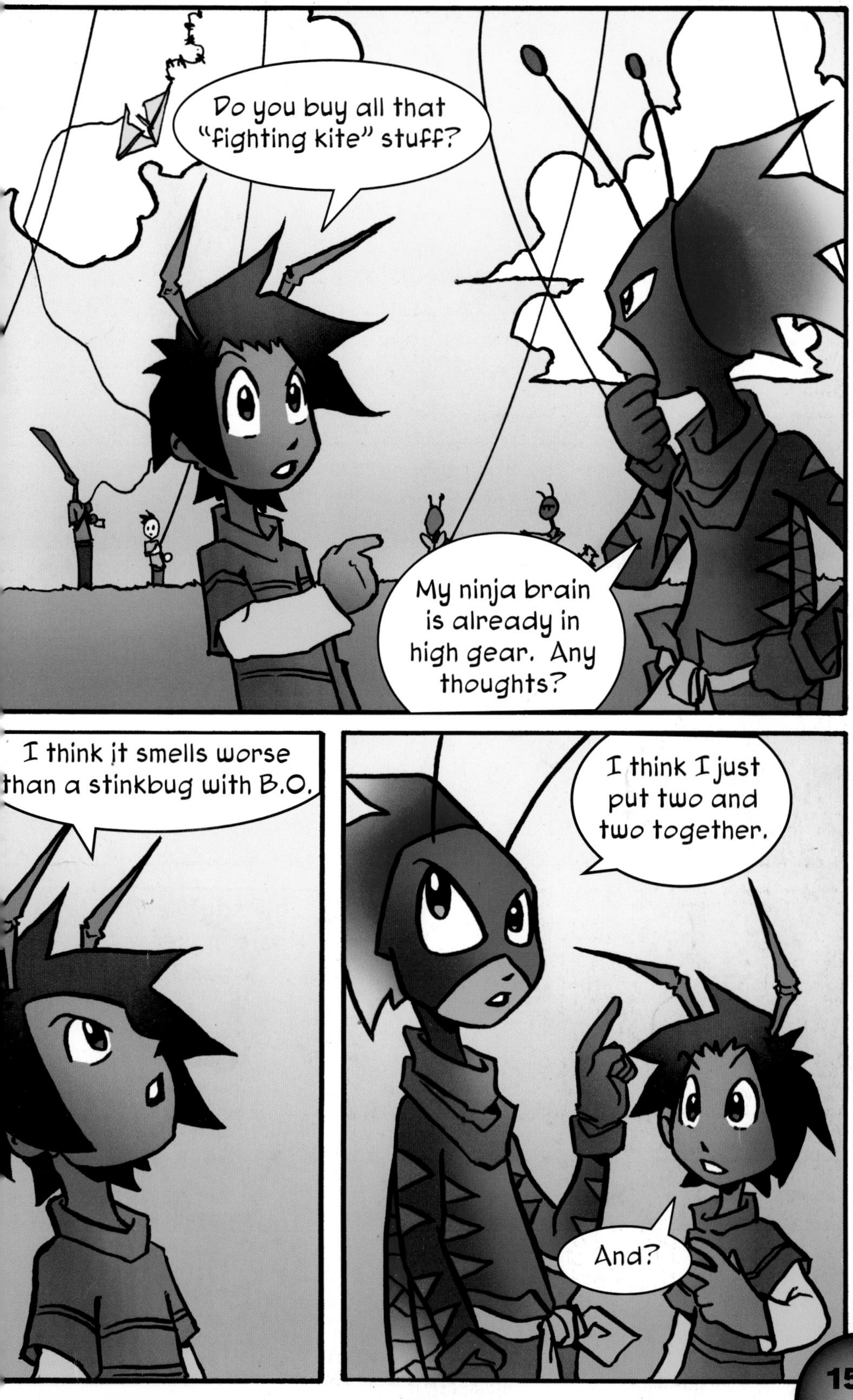
Do you buy all that "fighting kite" stuff?
My ninja brain is already in high gear. Any thoughts?
I think it smells worse than a stinkbug with B.O.
I think I just put two and two together.
And?

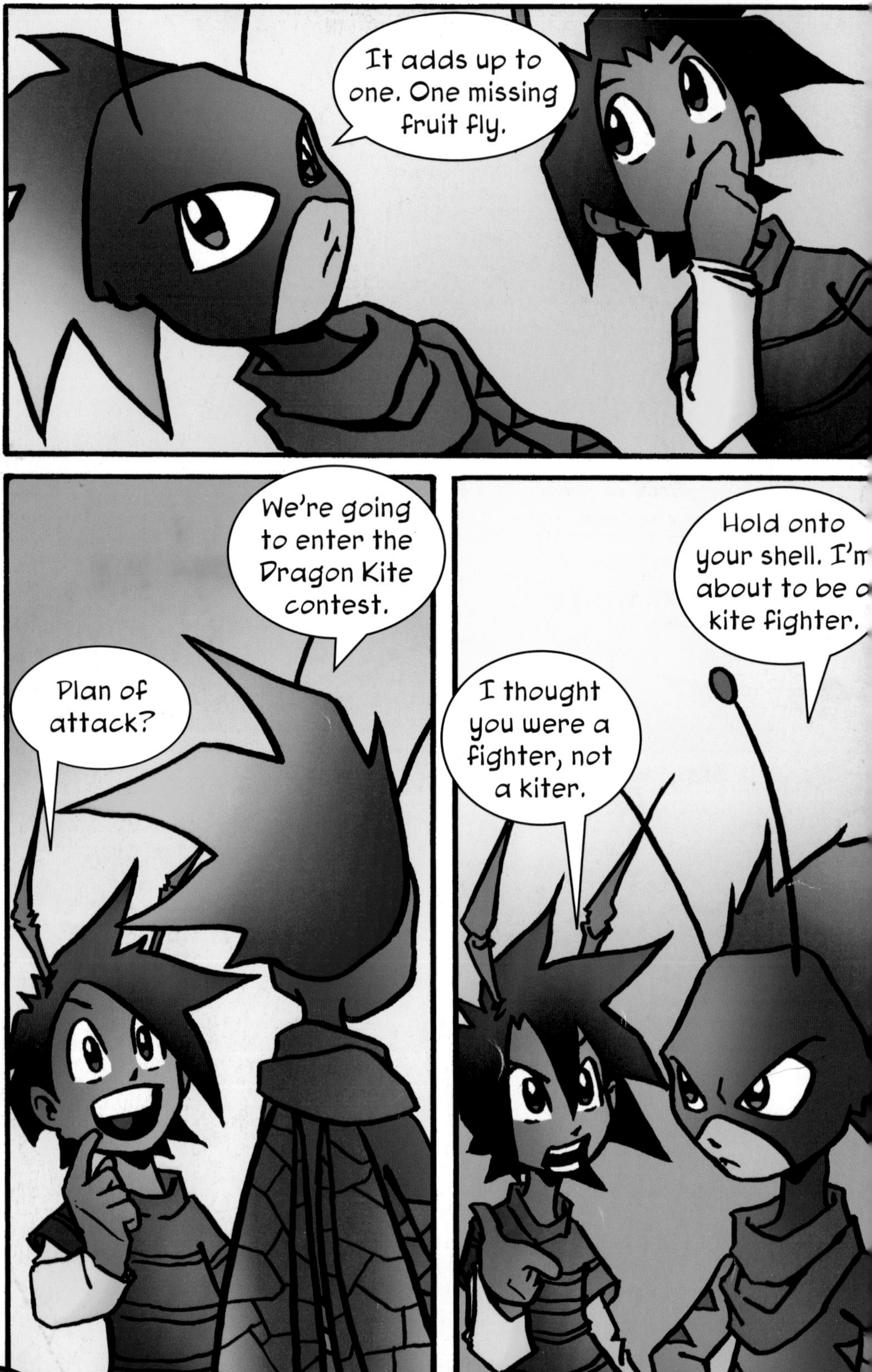

It adds up to one. One missing fruit fly.
Plan of attack?
We're going to enter the Dragon Kite contest.
I thought you were a fighter, not a kiter.
Hold onto your shell. I'm about to be a kite fighter.

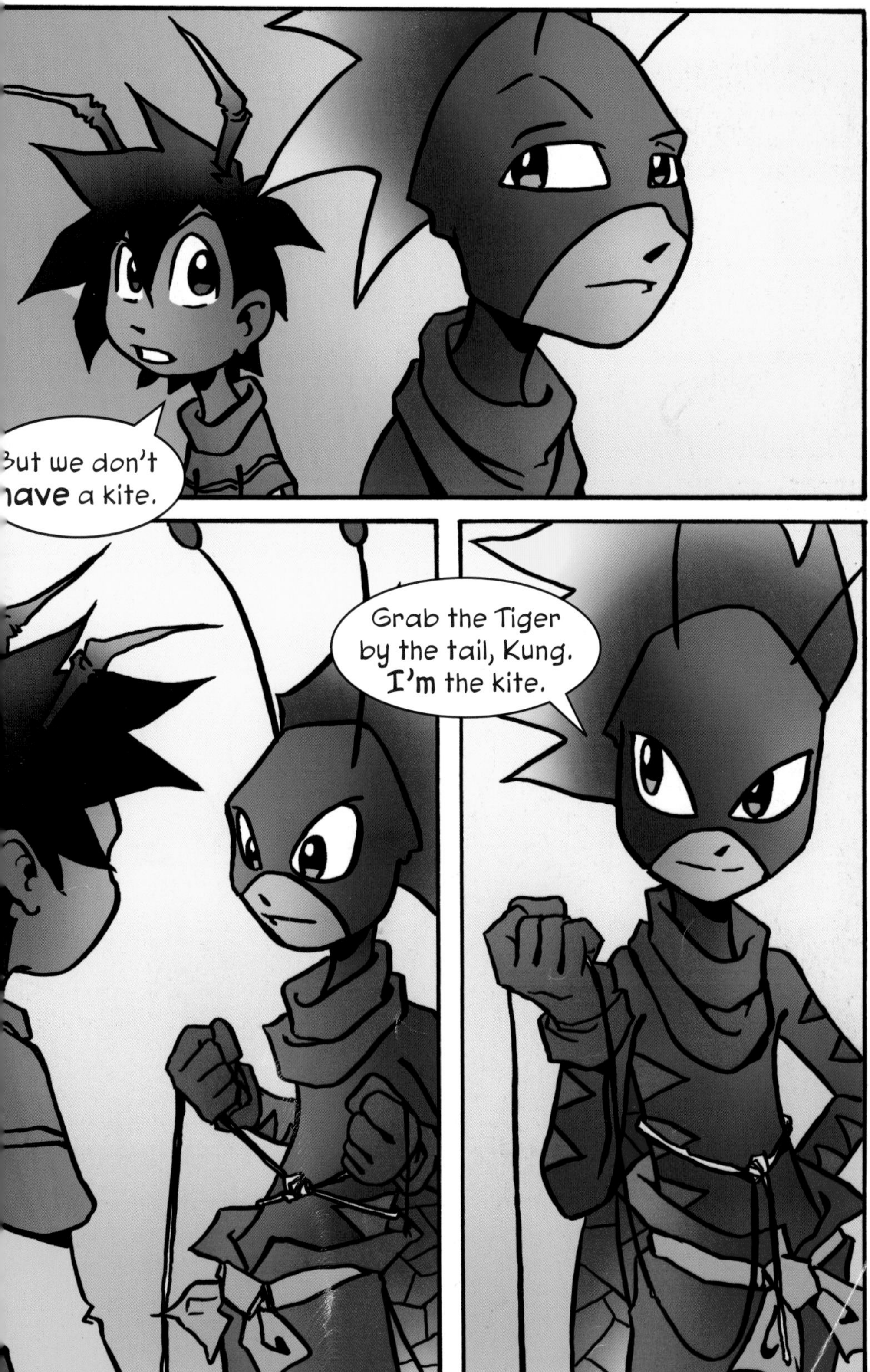
But we don't have a kite.
Grab the Tiger by the tail, Kung. I'm the kite.

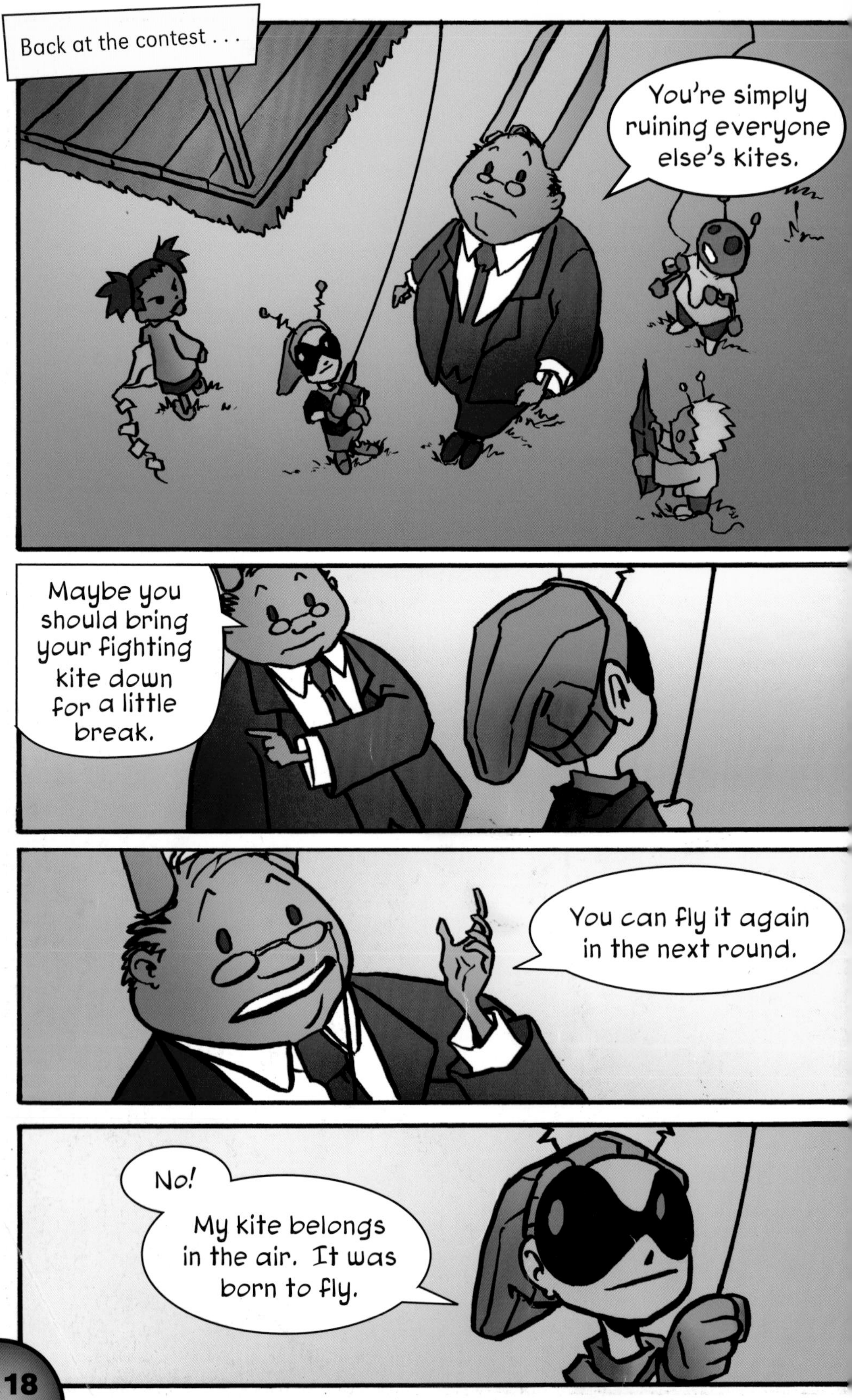

Back at the contest . . .
You're simply ruining everyone else's kites.
Maybe you should bring your fighting kite down for a little break.
You can fly it again in the next round.
No!
My kite belongs in the air. It was born to fly.

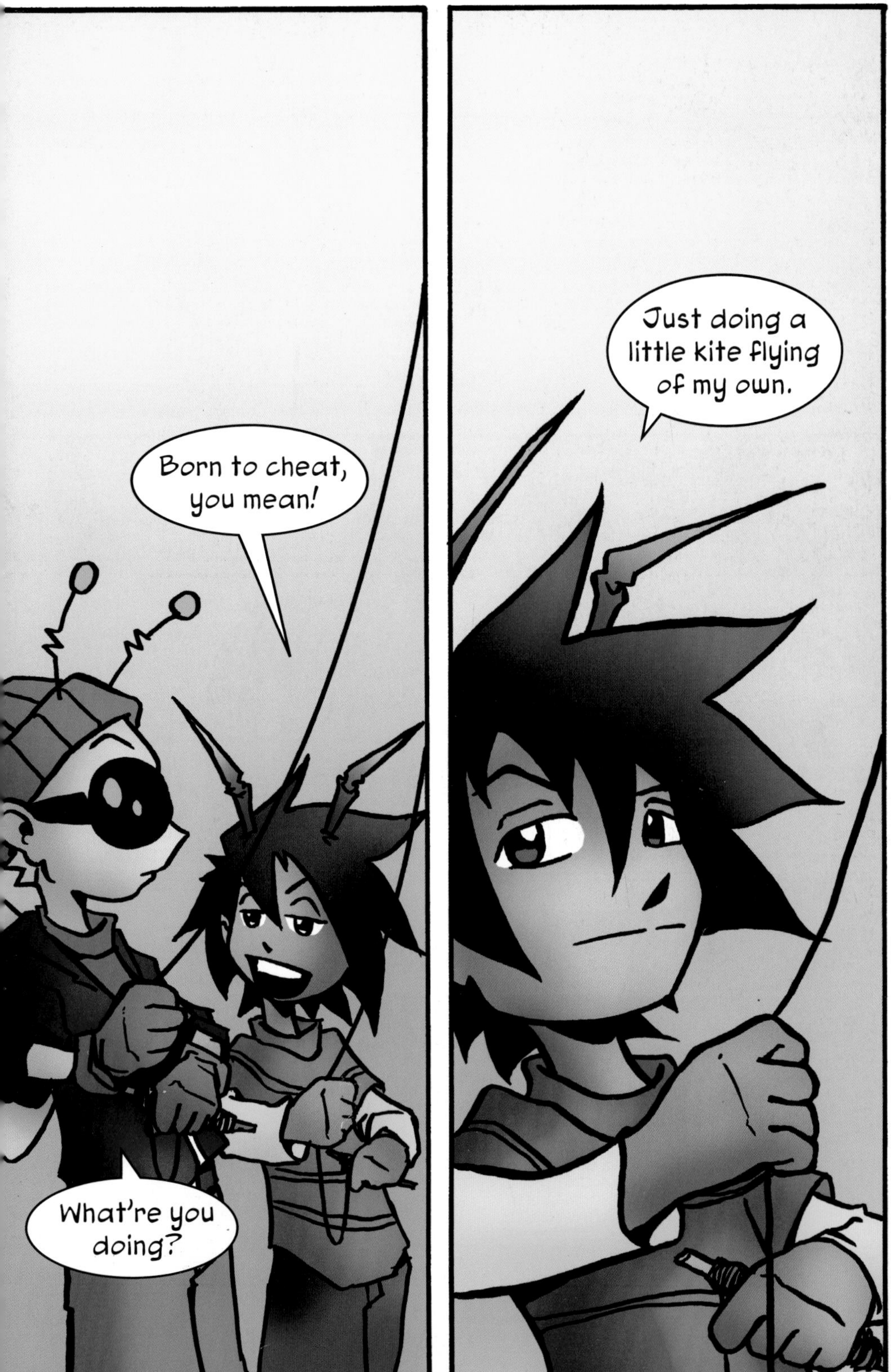
Born to cheat, you mean!
What're you doing?
Just doing a little kite flying of my own.

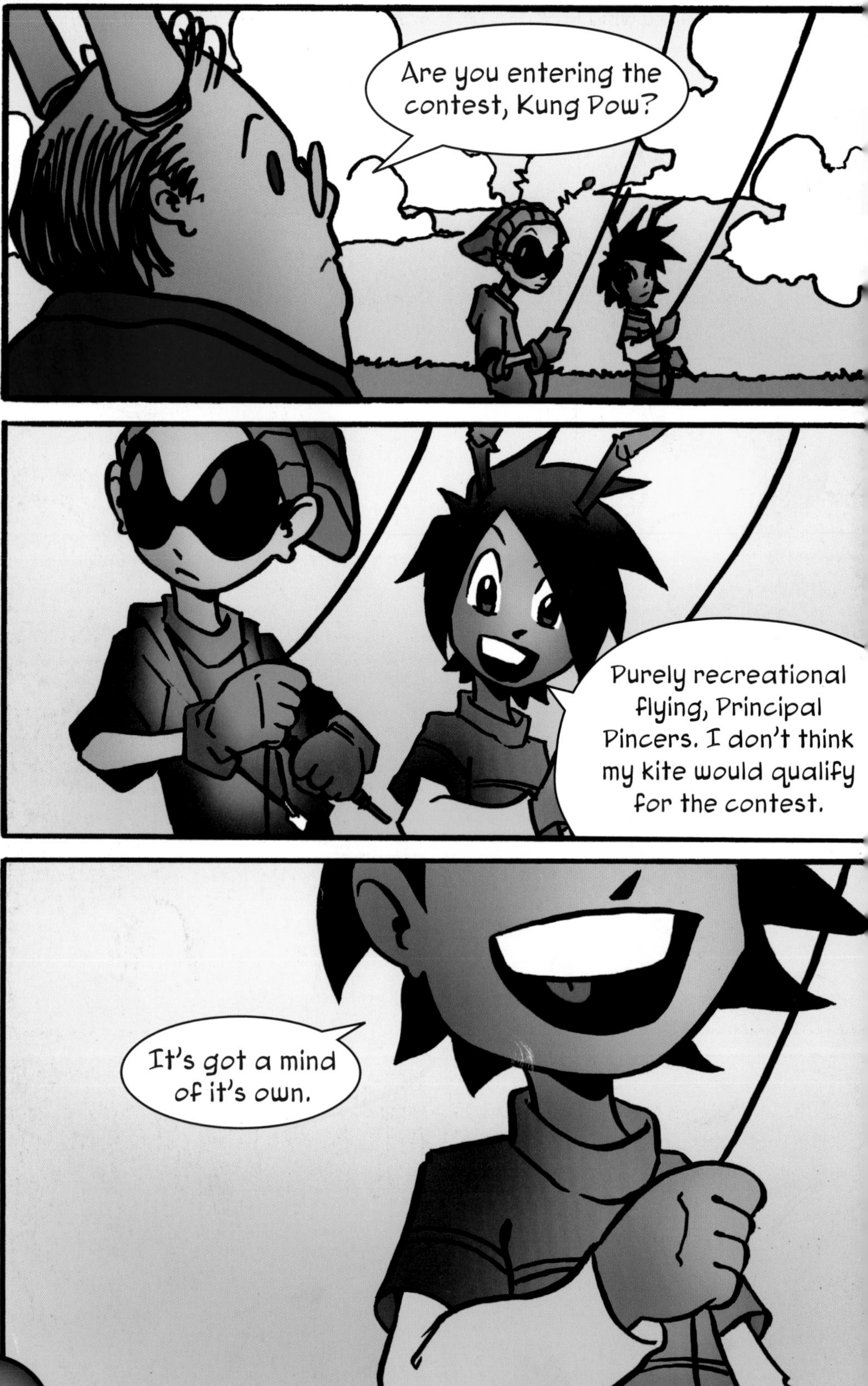
Are you entering the contest, Kung Pow?
Purely recreational flying, Principal Pincers. I don't think my kite would qualify for the contest.
It's got a mind of it's own.

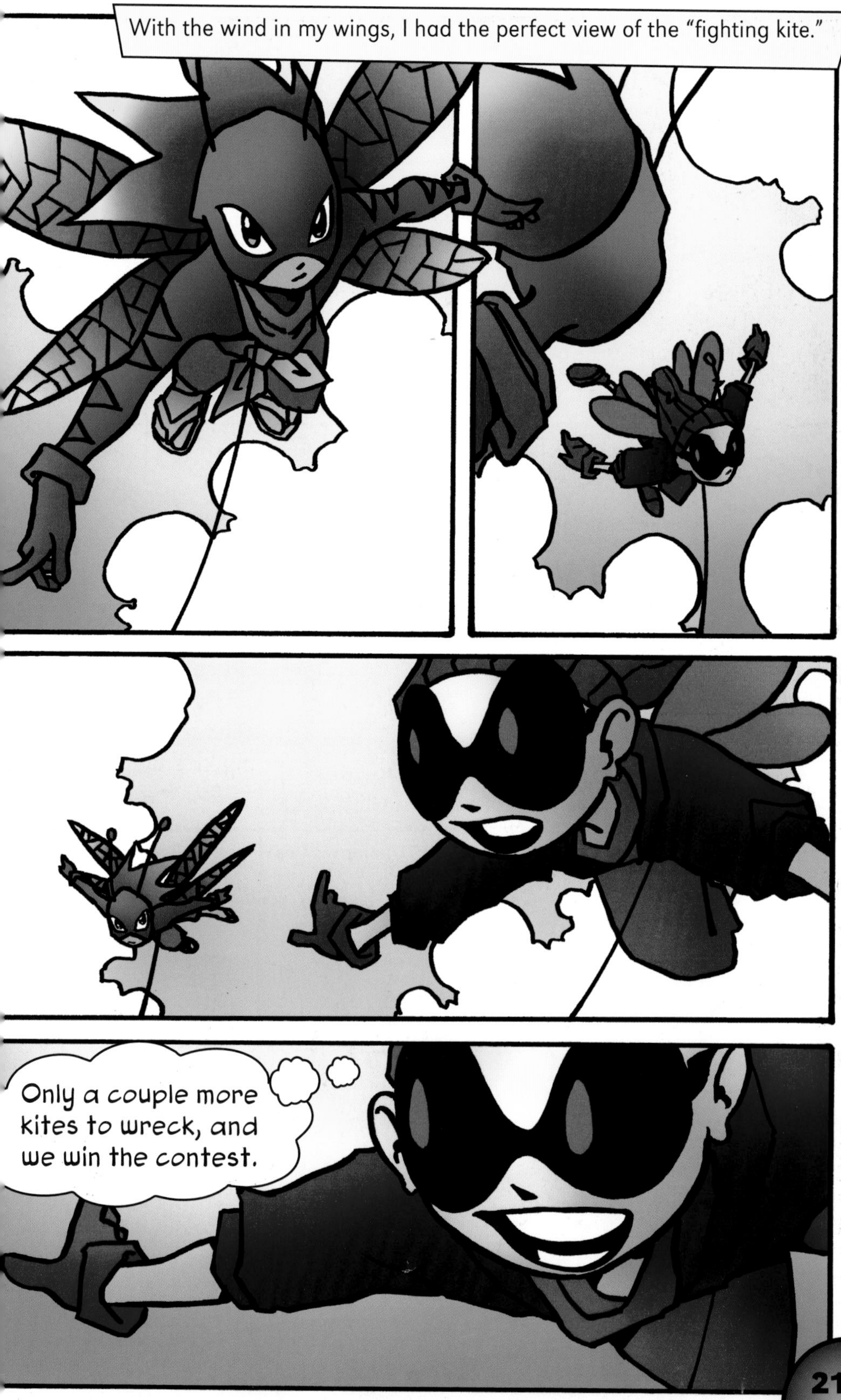
With the wind in my wings, I had the perfect view of the "fighting kite."
Only a couple more kites to wreck, and we win the contest.

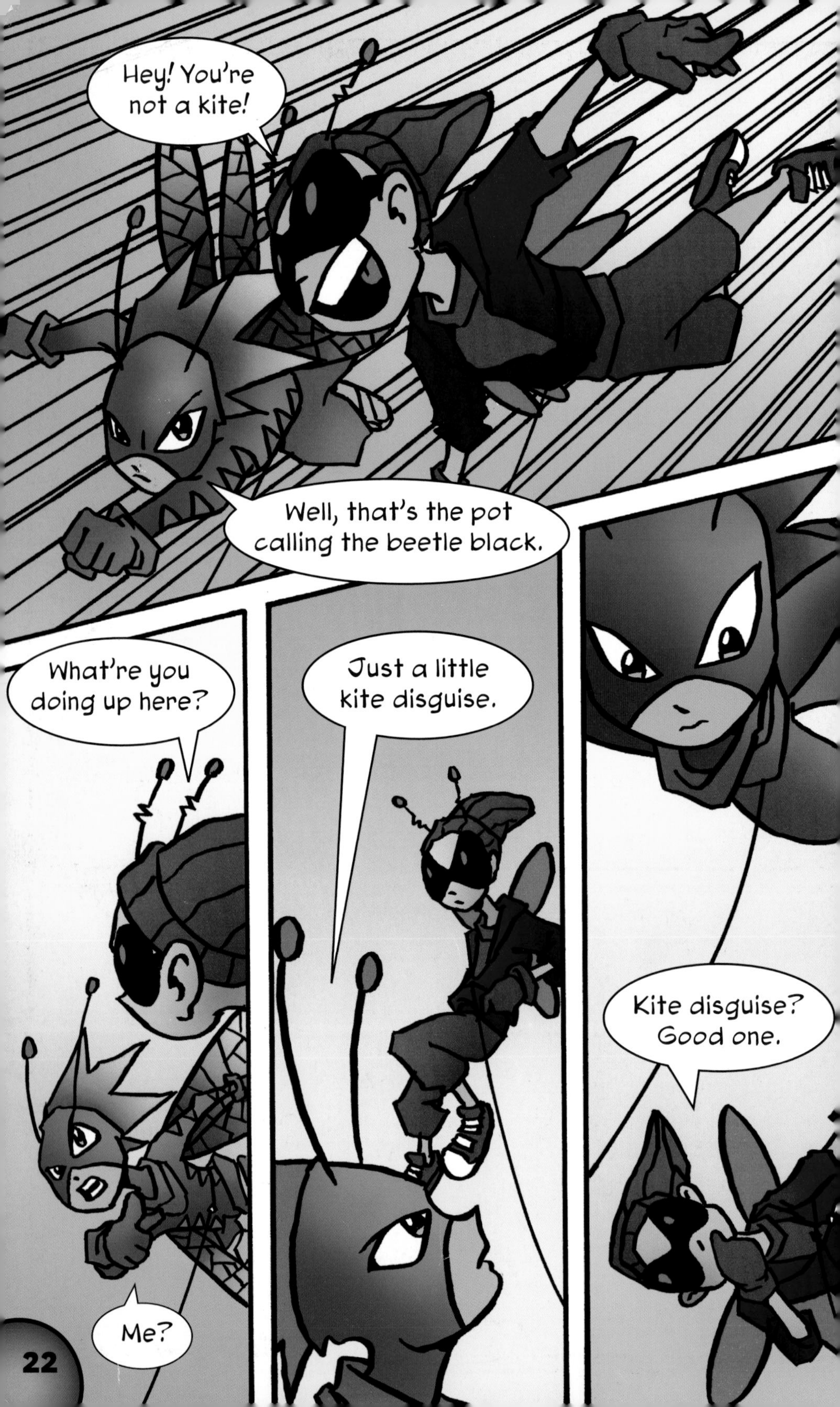
Hey! You're not a kite!
Well, that's the pot calling the beetle black.
What're you doing up here?
Me?
Just a little kite disguise.
Kite disguise? Good one.

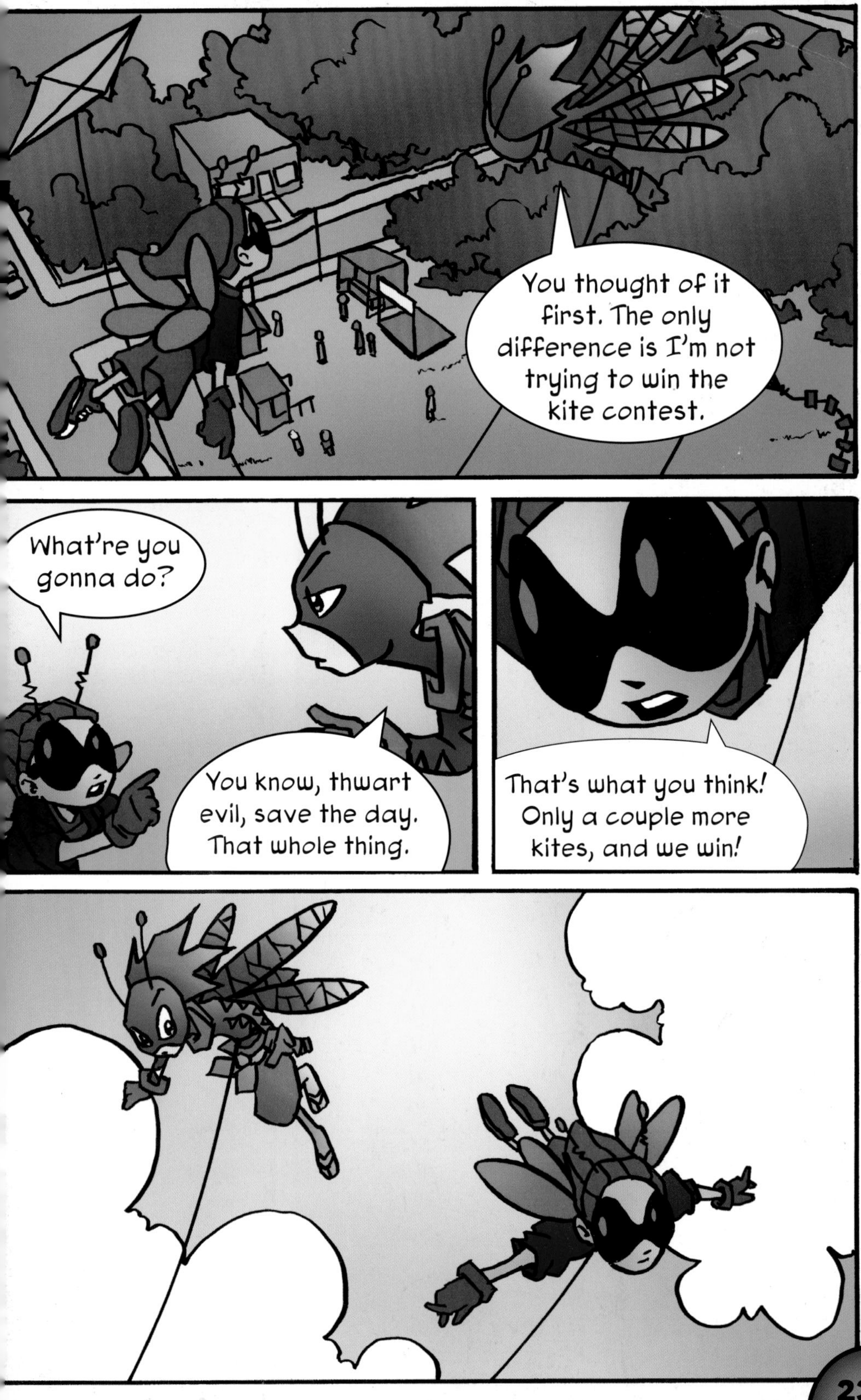

You thought of it first. The only difference is I'm not trying to win the kite contest.
What're you gonna do?
You know, thwart evil, save the day. That whole thing.
That's what you think! Only a couple more kites, and we win!

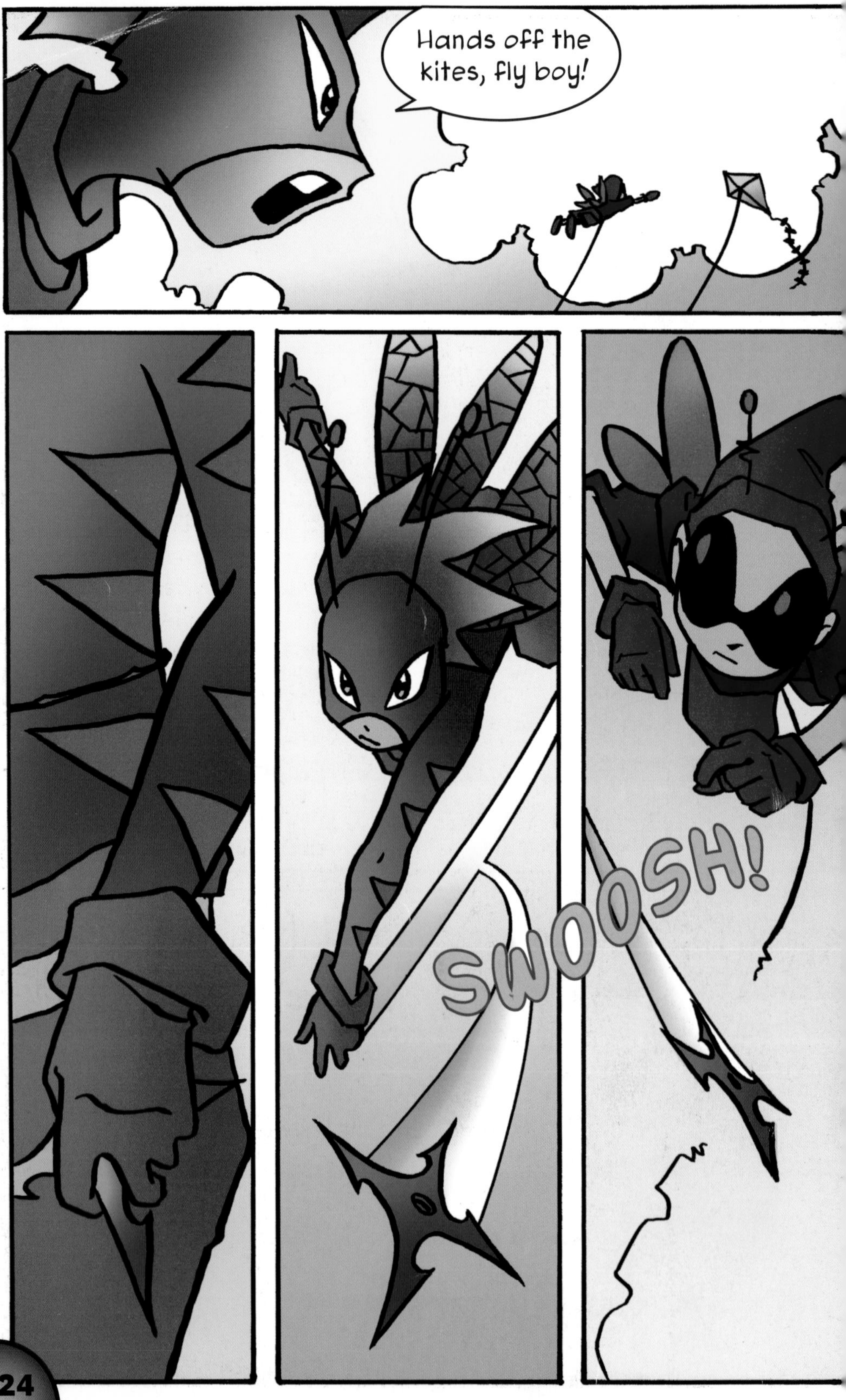
Hands off the kites, fly boy!
SWOOSH!

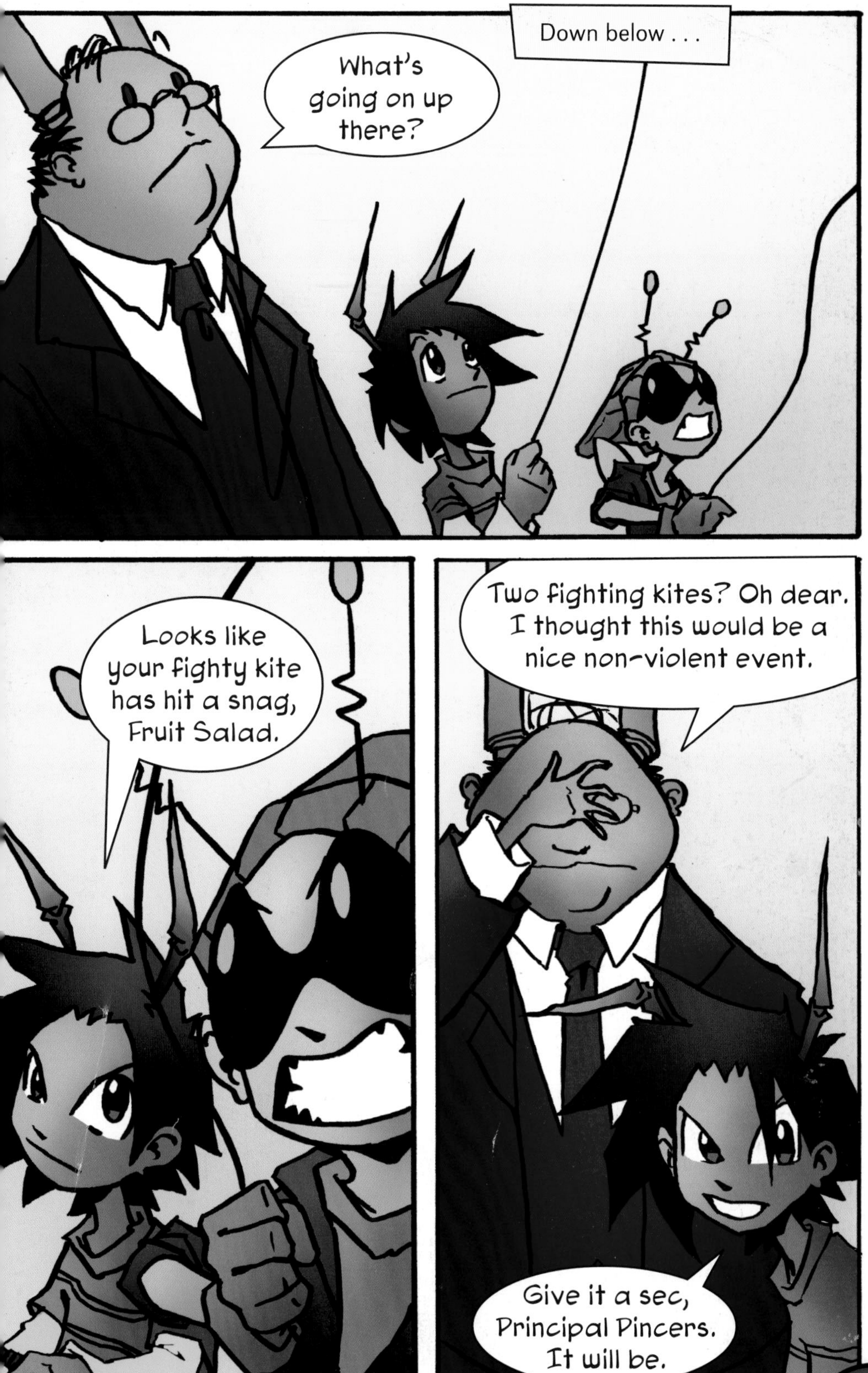
Down below . . .
What's going on up there?
Looks like your fighty kite has hit a snag, Fruit Salad.
Two fighting kites? Oh dear. I thought this would be a nice non-violent event.
Give it a sec, Principal Pincers. It will be.

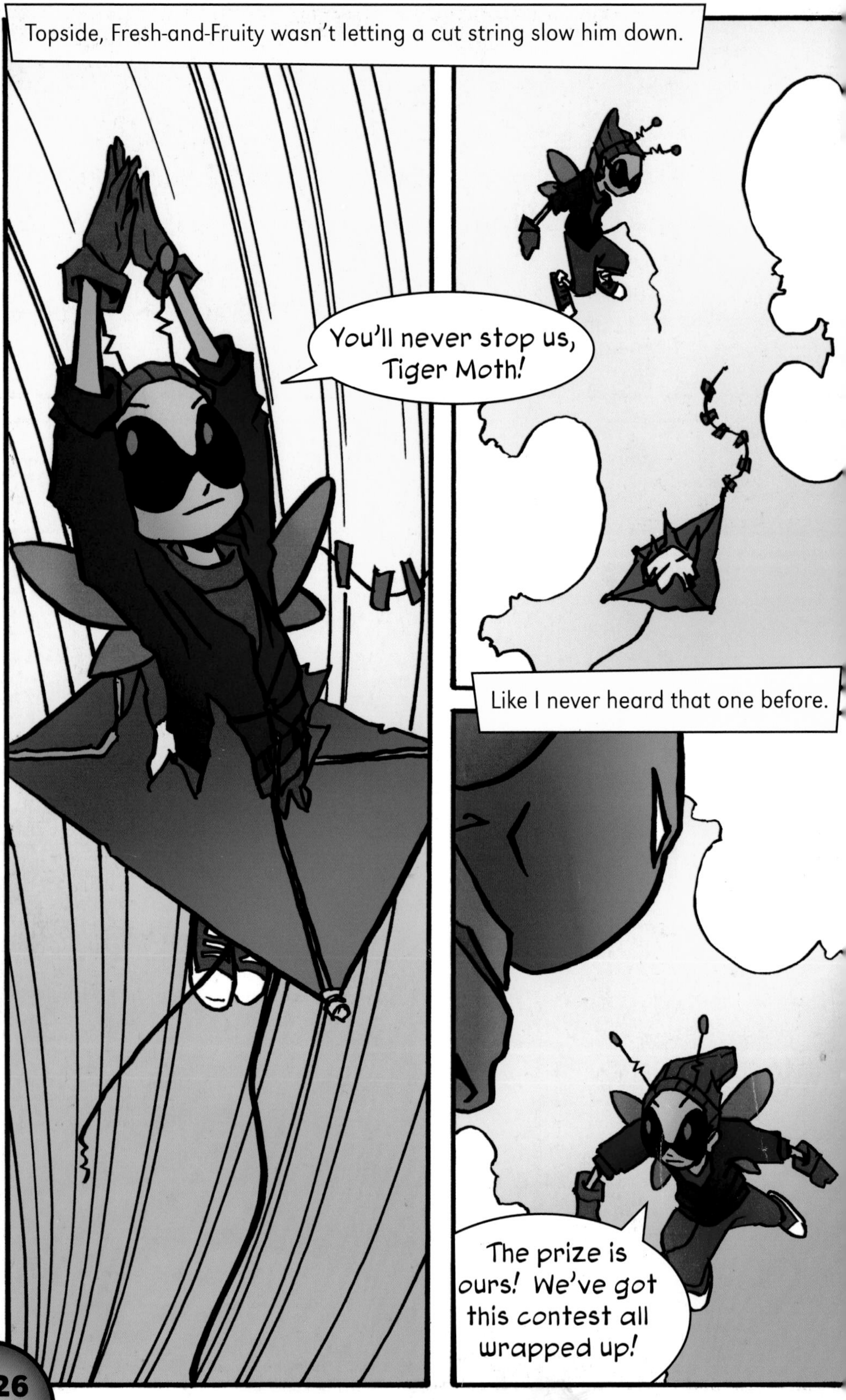
Topside, Fresh-and-Fruity wasn't letting a cut string slow him down.
You'll never stop us, Tiger Moth!
Like I never heard that one before.
The prize is ours! We've got this contest all wrapped up!

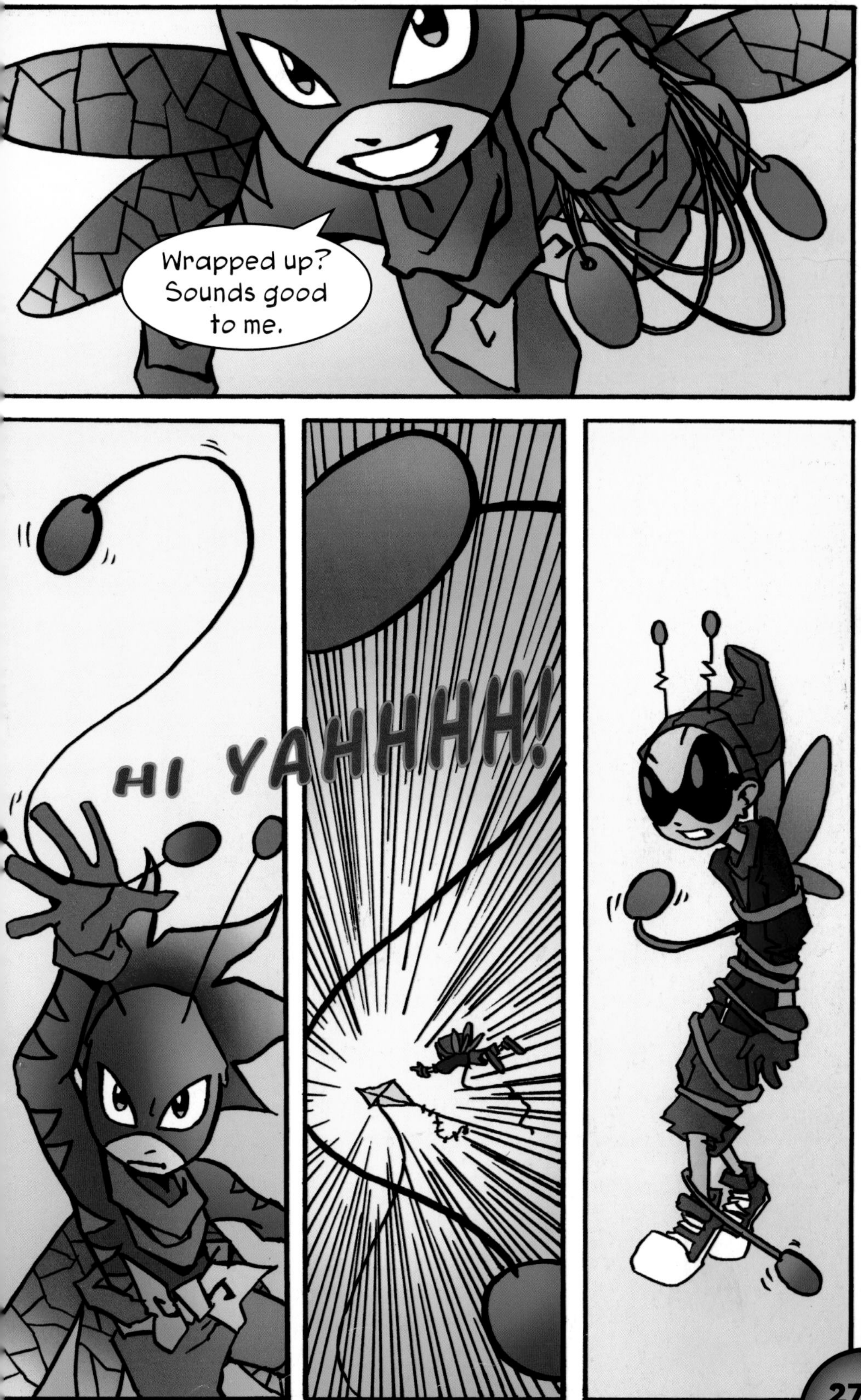

Wrapped up? Sounds good to me.
HI YAHHHHH!

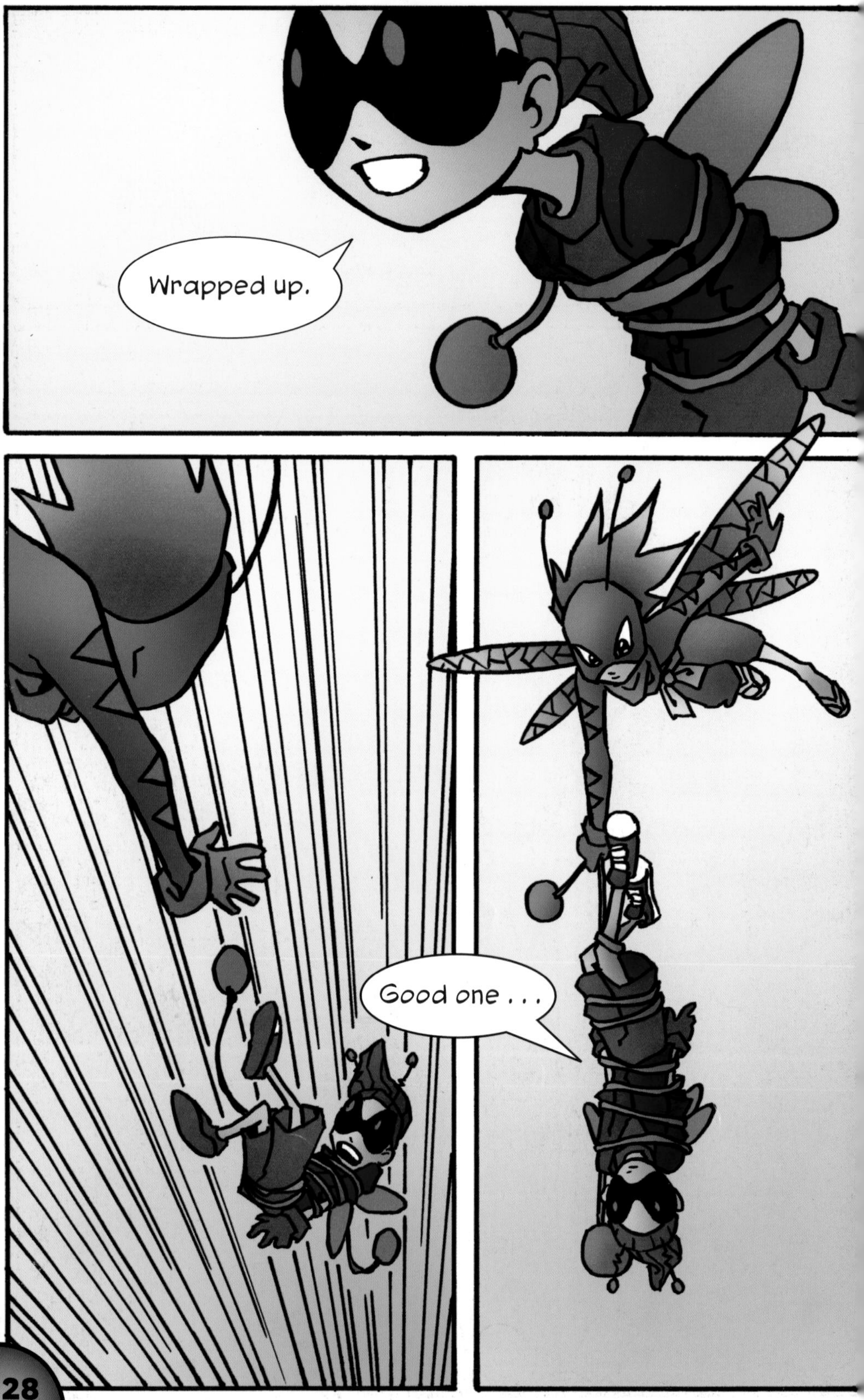
Wrapped up.
Good one . . .

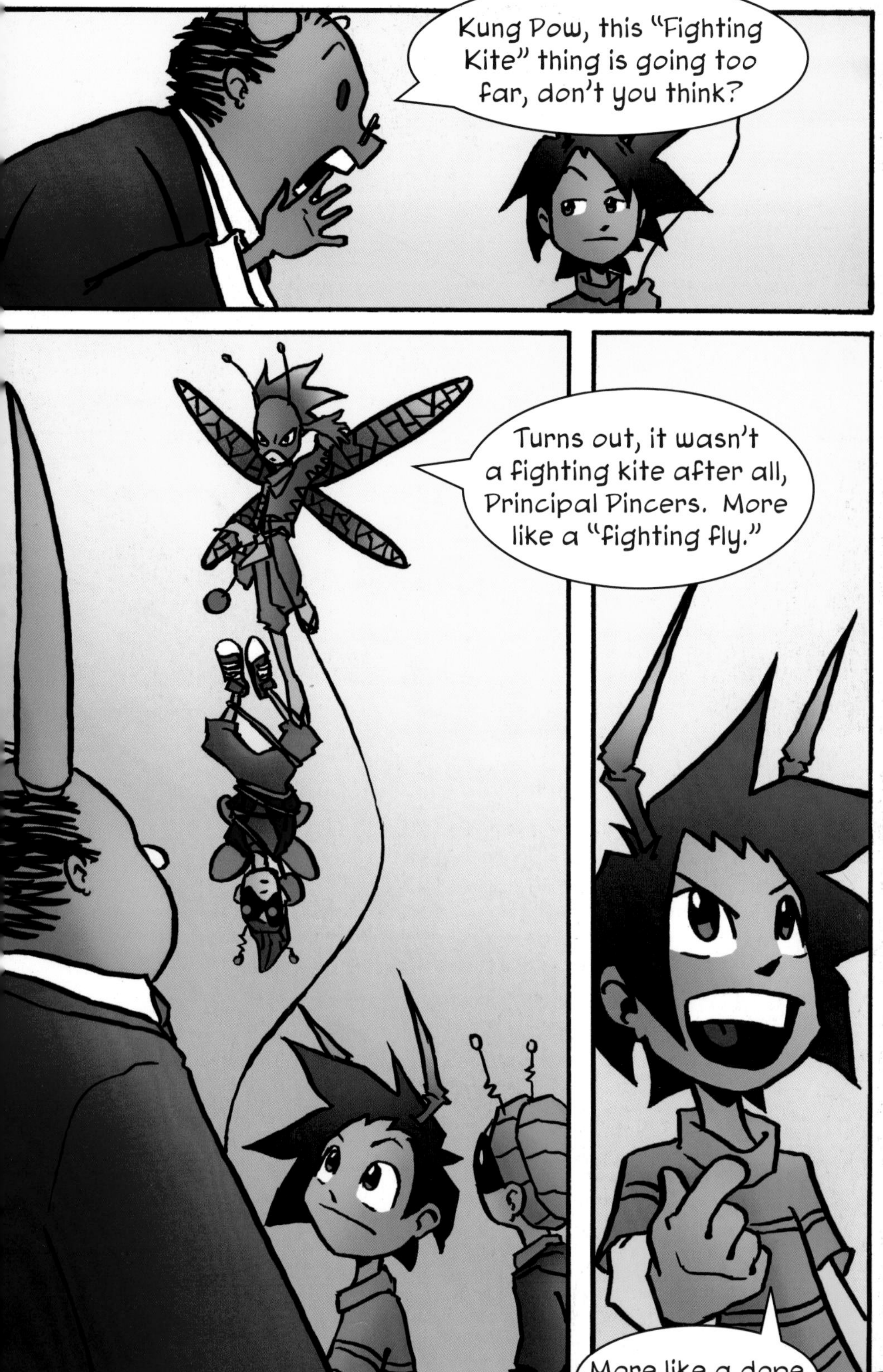

Kung Pow, this "Fighting Kite" thing is going too far, don't you think?
Turns out, it wasn't a fighting kite after all, Principal Pincers. More like a "fighting fly."
More like a dope on a rope.

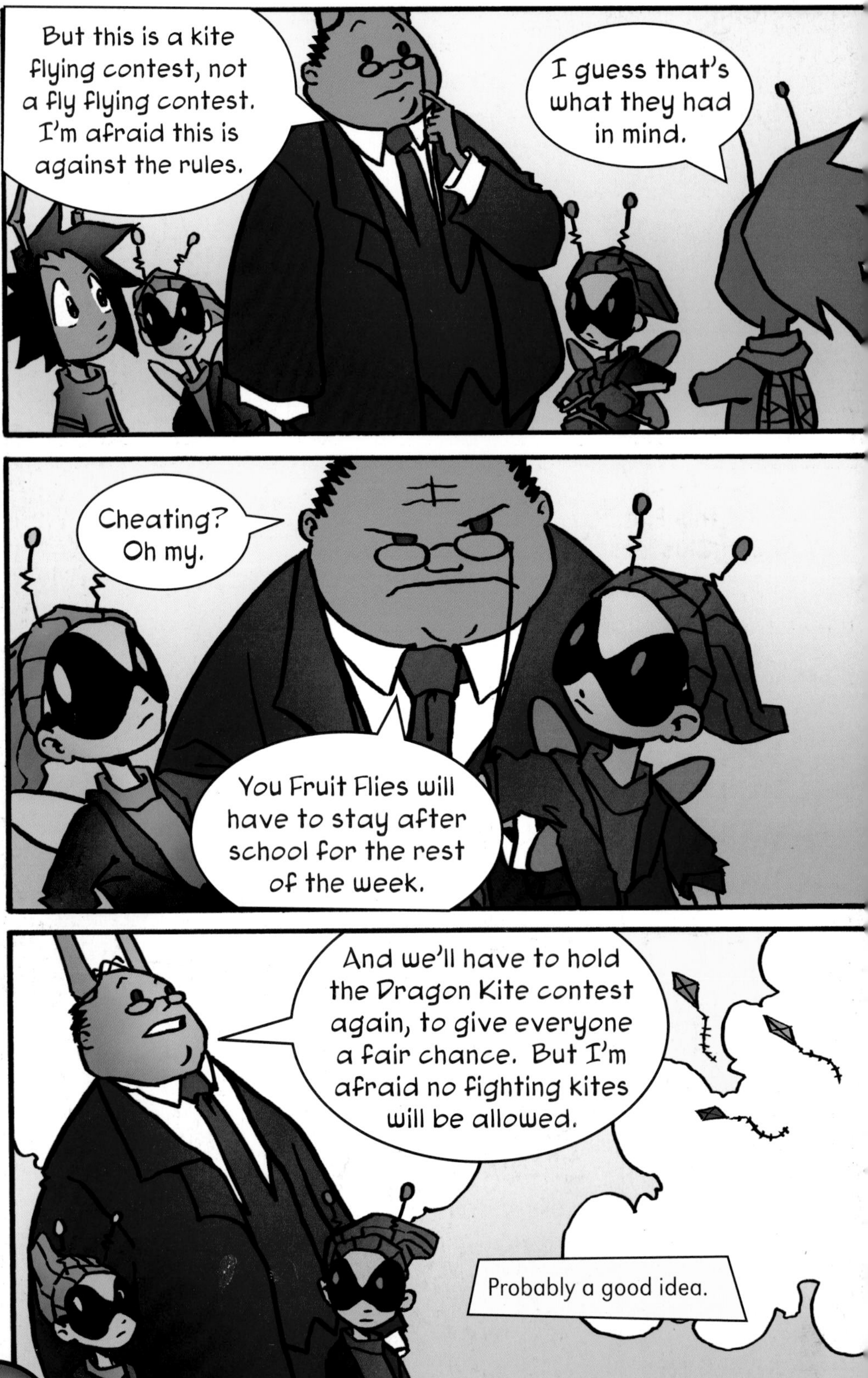

But this is a kite flying contest, not a fly flying contest. I'm afraid this is against the rules.
I guess that's what they had in mind.
Cheating? Oh my.
You Fruit Flies will have to stay after school for the rest of the week.
And we'll have to hold the Dragon Kite contest again, to give everyone a fair chance. But I'm afraid no fighting kites will be allowed.
Probably a good idea.

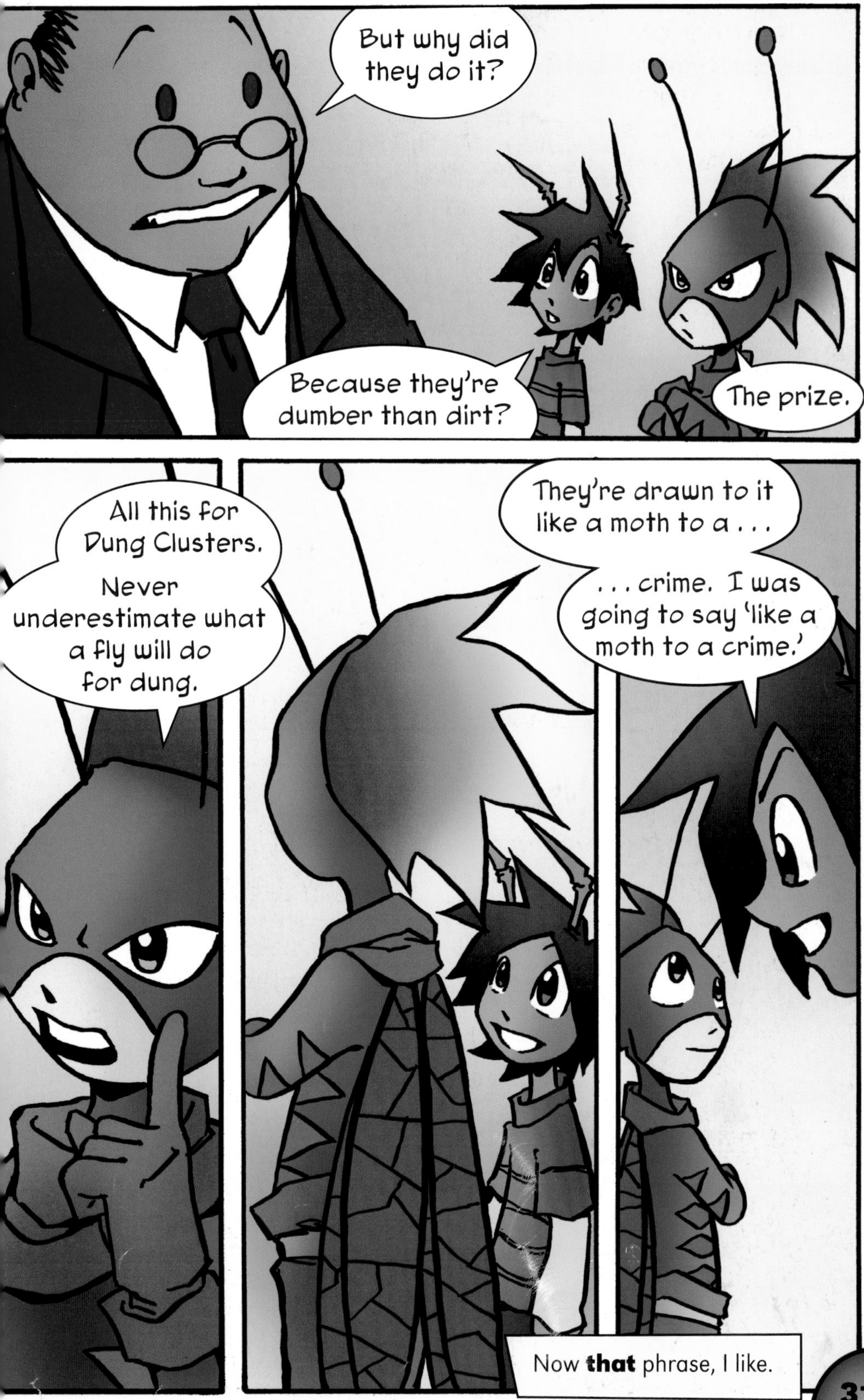
But why did they do it?
Because they're dumber than dirt?
The prize.
All this for Dung Clusters.
Never underestimate what a fly will do for dung.
They're drawn to it like a moth to a . . .
. . . crime. I was going to say 'like a moth to a crime.'
Now **that** phrase, I like.

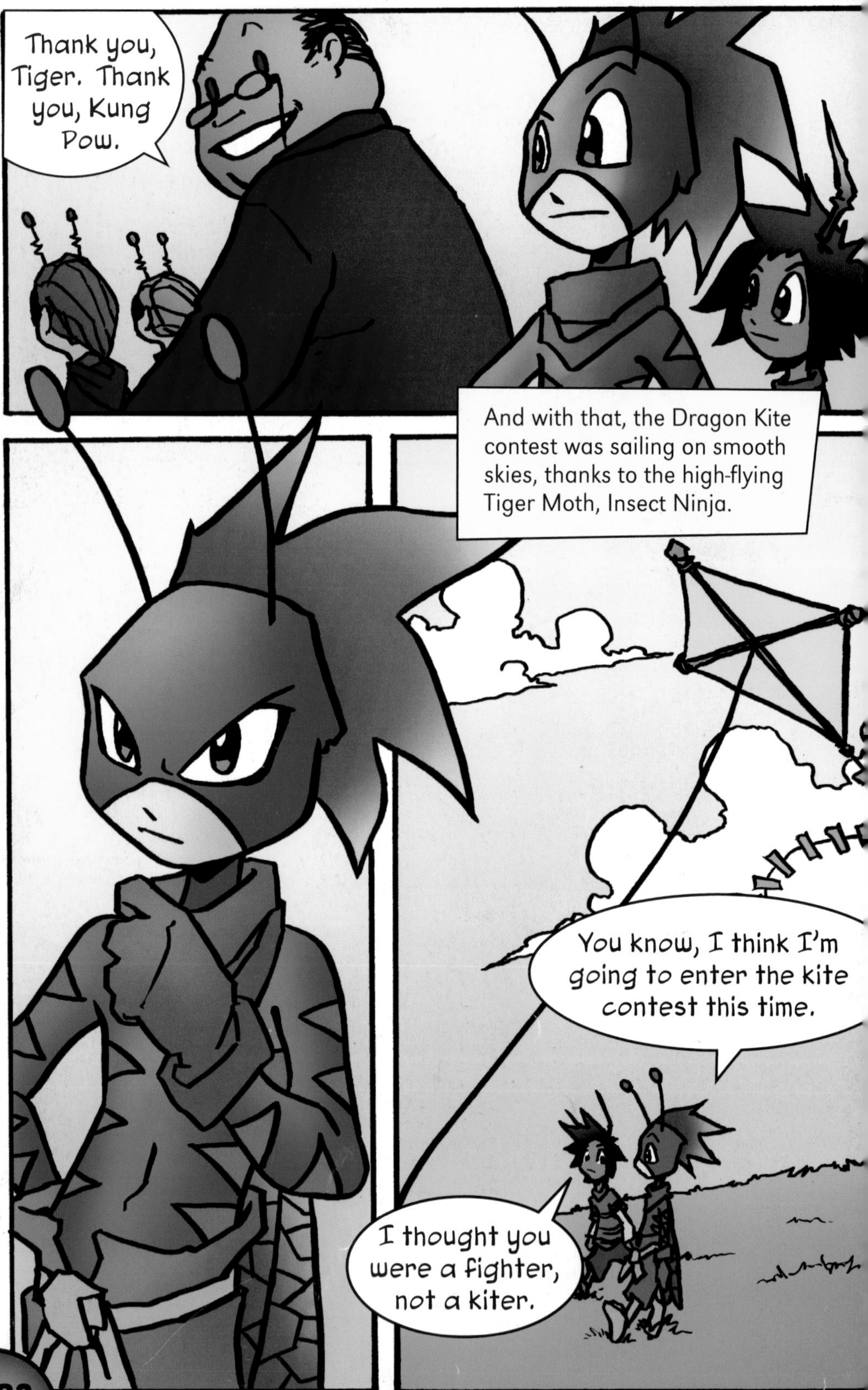
Thank you, Tiger. Thank you, Kung Pow.
And with that, the Dragon Kite contest was sailing on smooth skies, thanks to the high-flying Tiger Moth, Insect Ninja.
You know, I think I'm going to enter the kite contest this time.
I thought you were a fighter, not a kiter.

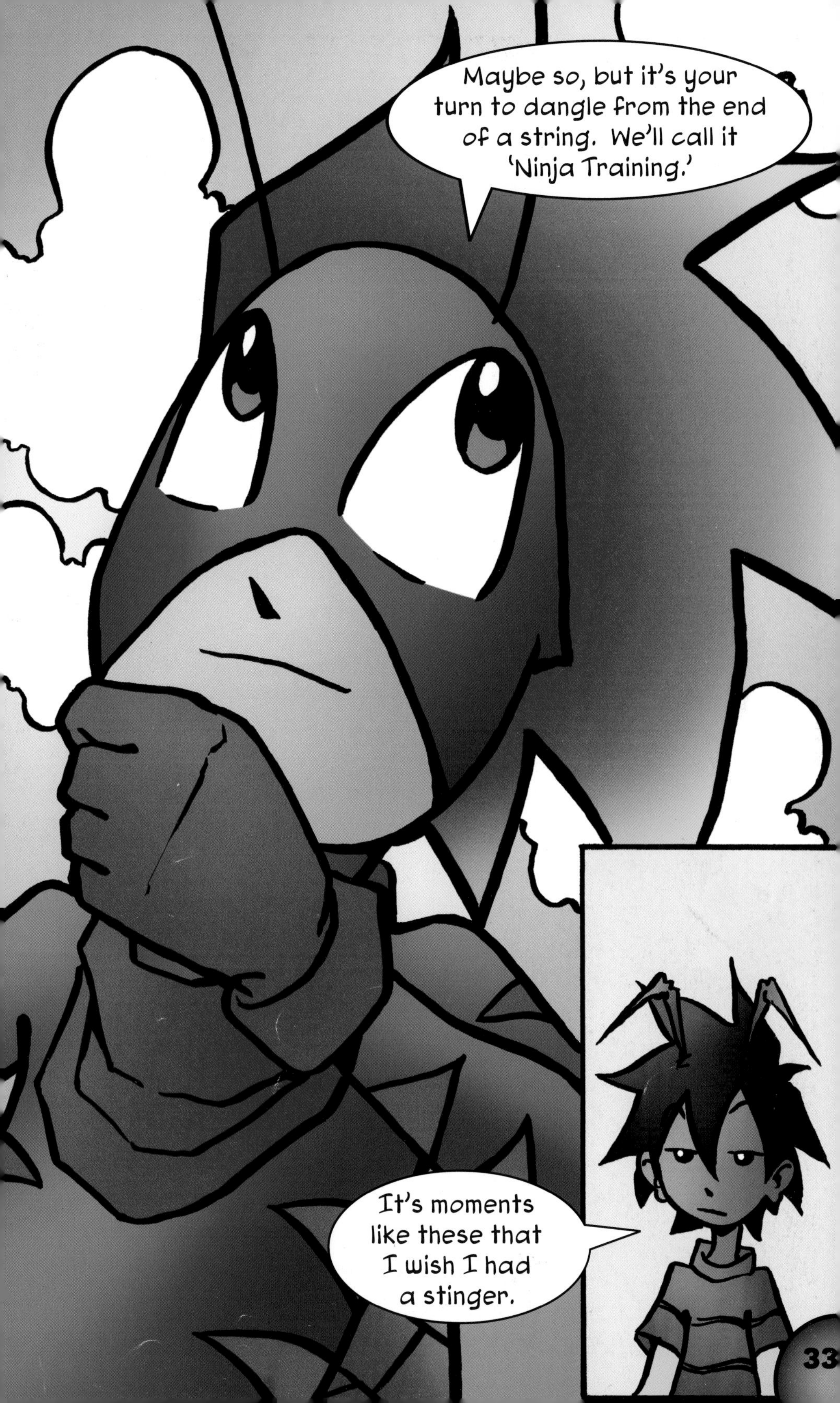
Maybe so, but it's your turn to dangle from the end of a string. We'll call it 'Ninja Training.'
It's moments like these that I wish I had a stinger.

ABOUT THE AUTHOR

Aaron Reynolds has never made a kite that would stay in the air for more than four seconds at a time. According to the Chinese New Year calendar, Aaron was born in the Year of the Dog. In spite of that, he likes cats and insects, but isn't the biggest fan of dung. Aaron is the author of the Tiger Moth series, Chicks and Salsa, and several other great books for kids. He lives near Chicago with his wife, two kids, and four slightly crazy cats.

ABOUT THE ILLUSTRATOR

Erik Lervold was born in Puerto Rico, a small island in the Caribbean, and has been a professional painter. He attended college at the University of Puerto Rico's Mayaguez campus, where he majored in Civil Engineering. Deciding that he wanted to be a full-time artist, he moved to Florida, New York, Chicago, Duluth, and finally Minneapolis. He attended the Minneapolis College of Art and Design, majored in Comic Art, and graduated in 2004. Erik teaches classes in libraries in the Minneapolis area and has taught art in the Minnesota Children's Museum. He loves the color green and has a bunch of really big goggles. He also loves sandwiches. If you want him to be your friend, bring him a roast beef sandwich and he will love you forever.

GLOSSARY

aerial (AIR-ee-uhl)—anything taking place in the air, like kite flying

B.O. (BEE-OH)—body odor, **stinky** body odor

dung (DUHNG)—animal droppings. Many insects feed on the nutrients found in animal dung.

mfft affff bptqqq (mfft-AFFFF-bptqqq)—a noise you make when you stuff your mouth with grapes

recreational (rek-ree-AY-shuhn-uhl)—an activity, usually a hobby, done purely for fun. This does not include picking on your little brother or sister.

rice paper (RYSS PAY-pur)—very thin, delicate paper used for decoration. If your homework is written on this paper, it is easier for your dog to eat it.

thwart (THWORT)—to keep someone from doing evil, such as cheating in a kite contest

FROM THE NINJA NOTEBOOK: SKY-HIGH FLYERS

Catch the wind, my fellow ninjas!

Kite building is an art form in China. The first Chinese kites were made from silk and bamboo three thousand years ago!

In 1903, Samuel Cody from Iowa crossed the English Channel in a canoe that was powered by huge kites. Cody also built giant kites that lifted him 2,000 feet into the air.

During the Hindu spring festival known as Basant, many families throughout Asia celebrate by flying kites.

Kites can be dangerous. Flyers in Pakistan and Afghanistan sometimes coat their kite strings with powdered glass. This makes the strings as sharp as razors. Flyers can then slice through an opponent's string during a kite fight.

The Megaray from New Zealand is considered by many experts to be the world's largest kite. It is 126 feet wide (42 meters), and covers an area of almost 7,000 square feet.

On the Southeast Asian island of Java, kites are used to catch food. Young men use kites armed with hooks to snatch flying bats out of the air!

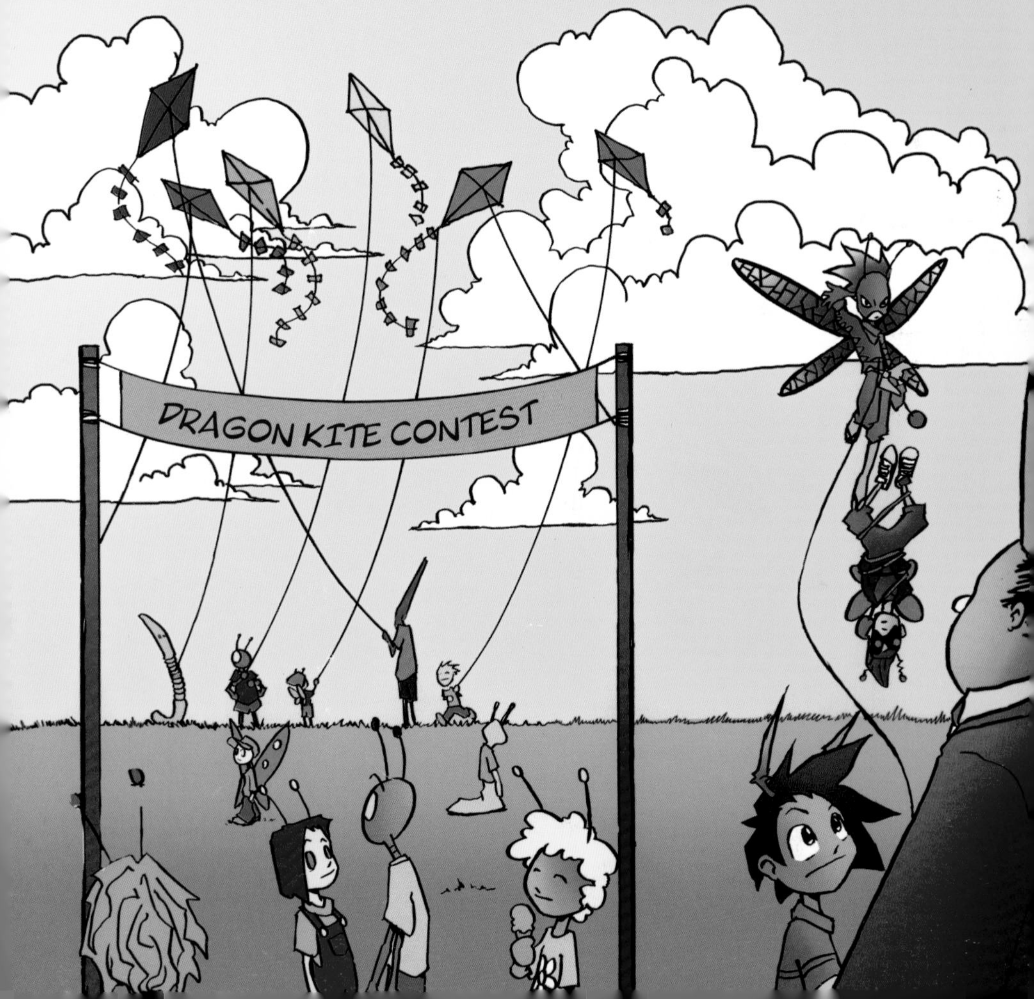
DRAGON KITE CONTEST

DISCUSSION QUESTIONS

1. Stories give us clues as we read along. What clues does this story give you about why Tiger Moth suspects the Fruit Fly Boys might try to cheat?

2. Where does most of the story take place? How is the setting different from other stories?

3. If you had friends like the Fruit Fly Boys who were always getting into trouble, what would you say to help them out? Why is it important for friends to help each other?

WRITING PROMPTS

1. Kite flying is a tradition on Chinese New Year. What are some of your family's traditions for the New Year? Why are traditions important? Write a story about a tradition that you like.

2. The Fruit Fly Boys cook up quite a scheme to win the kite contest. Have you ever planned to win something, only to have it backfire? If so what was it and what happened?

3. Pretend you're the main character, Tiger Moth. What is it like to fly in the sky like a kite? What do you see on the ground below? What do you see in the sky? Write a story told from Tiger Moth's point of view in the sky.

INTERNET SITES

Do you want to know more about subjects related to this book? Or are you interested in learning about other topics? Then check out FactHound, a fun, easy way to find Internet sites.

Our investigative staff has already sniffed out great sites for you!

Here's how to use FactHound:

1. Visit www.facthound.com

2. Select your grade level.

3. To learn more about subjects related to this book, type in the book's ISBN number: **1598890565**.

4. Click the **Fetch It** button.

FactHound will fetch the best Internet sites for you!